A Candlelight
Ecstasy Romance™

HE PULLED HER CLOSER, STARING INTENTLY AT HER LEFT HAND.

With reluctance she inhaled the clean male odor of his body. Overwhelmed, she jerked free of his hold as if on fire, scorched by the look in his smoldering eyes.

"You're more beautiful than I imagined," he whispered hoarsely.

"You—you recognized me?"

"Immediately! You look even more delectable with your silvery hair trailing down your back." Nick's husky voice lowered intimately as he scanned her figure without embarrassment. "I see no wedding or engagement ring. Are you available?"

"For what?"

"Me."

THE
SANDS OF
MALIBU

Alice Morgan

A CANDLELIGHT ECSTASY ROMANCE™

Published by
Dell Publishing Co., Inc.
1 Dag Hammarskjold Plaza
New York, New York 10017

Dell ® TM 681510, Dell Publishing Co., Inc.

Candlelight Ecstasy Romance™ is a trademark of
Dell Publishing Co., Inc., New York, New York.

ISBN: 0–440–18112–7

Printed in the United States of America
First printing—May 1982

Dear Reader:

In response to your continued enthusiasm for Candlelight Ecstasy Romances™, we are increasing the number of new titles from four to six per month.

We are delighted to present sensuous novels set in America, depicting modern American men and women as they confront the provocative problems of modern relationships.

Throughout the history of the Candlelight line, Dell has tried to maintain a high standard of excellence to give you the finest in reading enjoyment. That is and will remain our most ardent ambition.

Anne Gisonny
Editor
Candlelight Romances

THE
SANDS OF
MALIBU

CHAPTER ONE

Instinctively reacting to the siren's wail, Carlyn glanced in her rearview mirror. The ominous flashing red light gave her a moment's anxiety before she cautiously eased into the right-hand lane of Wilshire Boulevard. Deftly pulling to a stop in the first empty space, she parked her Volkswagen.

A smile tugged her soft lips as she waited for the officer to approach. Searching through the recesses of her shoulder purse, she found her billfold and removed her driver's license in preparation for the imminent confrontation.

Violet eyes sparkling with humor, she watched the forbidding figure of the officer as he parked his gleaming motorcycle behind her car, then lithely eased his leg over the black leather seat.

Dark glasses concealed his eyes beneath the white protective helmet emblazoned with the Los Angeles Police Department's emblem. The navy-blue uniform shirt was pegged skintight across his chest. Matching trousers hugged his thighs above knee-high boots polished glistening black to match the sheen of his Sam Browne belt and holster.

Ticket book in hand, he flipped back the cover as he approached the driver's side of the small car. He peered into the open window, his attitude grim, his voice serious, and asked to see her operator's license.

A petulant smile pursing her lips, Carlyn chuckled softly. "But . . . what did I do, Officer—er—" Noticing the three stripes on his sleeve: "Sergeant—" A quick glance to the chrome name tag over his right breast: "Broderick?"

He glowered, his hand reaching for Carlyn's license. "Impeded the flow of traffic, Miss Thomas. A flagrant violation of vehicle code number—"

"Darn you, Bill." She giggled. "You scared me to death, blaring that siren of yours. What's up?"

"My pulse rate from inhaling the sexy perfume you wear."

"Be serious, you goof!"

"I am serious. You were impeding traffic. I followed you for the last two miles and every red-blooded male in town did a double take when they saw your classy-looking face and that silvery mane of hair."

"Flatterer," she shot back, undaunted by his comments.

"Flattery nothing. It's the truth." Bill glanced sideways, returning the stare of the man who was watching them curiously while unlocking the door of his automobile parked in front of Carlyn's. With a shrug Bill bent down to Carlyn, whispering wryly, "See what I mean! That sophisticated-looking stud in the tailored three-piece suit is staring at you right now."

Unconcerned by the effect his words had on the stranger, Bill raised his voice, blatant remarks carrying clearly. "I'm due to go Code Seven now, Miss Thomas. Why don't I follow you to your pad? We could share dinner and still have half an hour left to indulge in some lusty indoor exercise before I return to duty." Leering mischievously, he added, "It'll save you from getting a ticket!"

Adamantly refusing Bill's request, Carlyn glanced forward, flushing briefly, her breath catching at the sight of the grimacing features of the arrogant-looking man bending to place a briefcase into his car. Their glances caught and held for a moment before he lowered his powerfully built form into the seat. Within seconds the sound of his Porsche pulling from the curb was drowned out by Bill's deep laughter as Carlyn continued to scold him.

"Didn't think you'd care for the idea, but thought it worth a query anyway. You're a classy-looking broad and my image would be tarnished if I went end of watch without at least one bribery attempt."

"You're ridiculous, Bill!" She laughed with good humor. "Your captain will probably get a citizen's complaint about your comments though." Her driver's license returned to her billfold, she looked up, laughing. "Let me go now, you big idiot. I have the next five days off and I don't want to waste a single minute. Five long days with nothing to do!"

Bill's warning to be good was followed by a sheepish grin when Carlyn reminded him to tell his wife and kids hello.

Seated on his cycle, legs braced, hand outheld to stop traffic, he waited for Carlyn to pull from the curb. He followed her for several blocks until he spotted, from the corner of his eye, a red sports car run a red light. Waving good-bye to Carlyn, he turned off onto Westwood Boulevard in pursuit of the legitimate traffic violation. All thoughts of Carlyn left his mind as he settled quickly into the serious routine of his sometimes dangerous job.

The bright sun beating down on the city, Carlyn continued driving, not even feeling the heat. Her mind was preoccupied by her plans. A sigh of pleasure escaped her lips as she entered her cool West Los Angeles apartment, colorfully decorated with discriminating taste. She walked directly through the living room to her bedroom and set her purse on the nightstand next to the wide bed—a chaste bed that was unshared by any of the men she occasionally dated. They were persistent but soon learned she was not interested in casual affairs.

Habit born of responsibility guided her hands as she removed the small two-inch Smith and Wesson thirty-eight caliber revolver from her uniform purse. Sliding the built-in closet doors aside, she reached for a heavy metal box high on the upper shelf. She placed her gun inside and locked it securely, then changed into casual clothes, planning to spend the evening relaxing after the stress of her demanding job.

Early the next morning Carlyn stood quietly admiring her bright kitchen, while inhaling the lemony smell of the freshly scrubbed floor. Wiping her hands on the sides of snug-fitting jeans, she brushed a tendril of wavy hair from her damp forehead. With an excess of energy she had decided to use a brush rather than a mop.

Maple-stained shutters on each side of the wide window shone with polish beneath a brown calico-print ruffle. Potted ivy spilled a profusion of green leaves over the window-sill. Cooking utensils propped in a fat ceramic crock and amber glass canisters were vivid against the beige tile counter and, along with copper-bottom pans, added to the homey atmosphere of her sunny kitchen.

The phone rang shrilly, in discord with the plaintive refrain of the Olivia Newton-John tape playing on the stereo. Carlyn lifted the receiver, her eyes bright with pleasure as she recognized her sister-in-law's voice.

"Gosh, am I glad you're home. Got any days off?"

"Five."

"Excellent. Bob and I had to cut our vacation short, so you can take our place. His boss will be in D.C. for a few more weeks and prefers his house is occupied. I still can't believe it! The first opportunity to stay in a millionaire's home free and our two kids get sick. We went from luxury to diapers and baby aspirin in one hour."

"Too bad. How do they feel now?" Carlyn inquired with loving concern for her niece and nephew. Aware of Marianne's knack for long conversations, she curled comfortably against the cushions of her favorite velour chair.

"Fine!" Marianne answered with exasperation. "Those two are tough as old boots. Our baby-sitter panicked unnecessarily when Betsy ran a mild temperature. Not wanting to be outdone by his sister, Billy complained of a tummyache. Forget those little devils. Pack your sexiest bikini and drive to Malibu as fast as possible."

"It sounds fun, but I don't know—"

Interrupting, Marianne blurted out, "Wait until you see the house, Carlyn. It's a dream come true. Ultramodern, with glass walls and wide decks jutting out right over the beach. It's a perfect bachelor pad for sunning and sinning!" She giggled suggestively. "King-size beds, marble bath big enough for two, and a sensuous fur rug sprawled in front of a huge fireplace."

Carlyn gazed with appreciation at her apartment. She had decorated it with carefully selected furniture and quality accent pieces that complemented her feminine personality. Curious to see how the affluent lived, she thought the opportunity to stay in a luxurious mansion was irresistible. "Okay, I'll do it!" she agreed impulsively.

"Fantastic! Leave your inhibitions behind though. I hate to lecture again but you really are a prude, love. If I were single, had sexy violet eyes, and a knockout figure like yours, I wouldn't be a twenty-five-year-old virgin."

"Not again, Marianne . . . please. I'm perfectly happy." Carlyn smiled to herself as she listened to another outspoken opinion about her outdated morals and continued reluctance for intimate involvement with a man.

"With your occupation, Carlyn, you should be particularly aware how liberated women are now. I'm not saying

15

you should be promiscuous, but there's certainly no stigma in having one or two passionate love affairs. Why, it isn't even healthy to suppress your normal sexual needs."

Undaunted by the blunt comments, Carlyn replied firmly, "My old-fashioned principles don't bother me in the least. I've certainly never been tempted to lower them to gratify the heightened desires of some groping, heavy-breathing male!"

"There's your problem. You've never been tempted. Despite your work as a policewoman your personal life is almost cloistered. It's just not natural."

Both shapely legs curled beneath her, Carlyn let her mind wander, anticipating her sudden plans with pleasure. Her soft laughter stopped Marianne's chatter when she reminded her mischievously, "Remember your last attempt to find me a partner in passion? He nearly had heart failure when you told him I worked for the Los Angeles Police Department. He could hardly wait to leave for fear I'd find out about his unpaid traffic fines and arrest him at the dinner table. Besides, despite your derision, I have all the social life I desire."

"I guess he wasn't the right man for you," Marianne sighed.

Carlyn's soft voice lowered as she added seriously, "If you want the truth, I find very few men capable of handling the fact that a female can be better qualified physically and mentally than they are. Another thing that puts them off is my salary. The L.A.P.D. is the highest-paid police force in the United States, and I earn more than most of the men I meet. It's nearly impossible to find a man who acts natural in my presence once he finds out what my occupation is."

"Don't tell them, then, silly. There's no need to confess your life history during your first few dates," Marianne scolded. "Get going so you can start enjoying yourself, and for crying out loud, if you meet some macho guy, don't tell him what you do. Pretend you're a secretary or something else more normal than a police officer."

Stretching her long slender legs in front of her, Carlyn chuckled, gleaming tendrils of silvery blond hair cascading around her shoulders in startling contrast to the navy-blue of her T-shirt. "Great idea! I'll completely forget I'm a police officer devoted to protecting and serving the people of L.A., but remember, I'm more interested in getting a tan than hunting for a man on the make."

"Darn it, Carlyn, if it wasn't for me constantly searching for a suitable man for you, you'd probably end up an old maid. You aren't even interested in those handsome policemen you work with."

"I was just propositioned by one of those 'handsome policemen.' Like most of the others, he is married too. A good reason, I think, to eliminate most policemen from my list of eligible males."

A half smile on her lips, she continued. "Regardless, why should I want to get married now anyway? I doubt if there is a job with more interest or challenge for a woman than mine. I never know one day to the next what assignment I might be given, plus I thoroughly enjoy the work. What could any man possibly offer me that is better than what I have now?"

"The fact that you have to ask is what bothers me the most. You talk like a self-reliant woman, Carlyn," Marianne scolded firmly. "But remember, you never do anything by half measures. When you fall in love, you'll give your very soul to the man of your choice. You, my dear beautiful sister-in-law, will completely flip your untouched generous heart and I can hardly wait to see it happen!"

"You're hopeless. Hang up so I can pack. I promise to keep my eyes open for a hairy-chested, brawny hero. Someone tall, dark, and handsome sounds ideal." Unbidden, the image of the glaring stranger came to her mind.

The width of his powerful shoulders, the arrogant tilt of his proud chin, his gleaming raven-black hair, his piercing eyes locking with hers—she saw him clearly. Handsome beast, she admitted reluctantly before forcing him from her thoughts.

Marianne took Carlyn's teasing words seriously, telling her to call the minute she got back. "Oh, by the way, the keys are under the front doormat."

Carlyn's groan at Marianne's ignorance, after all the warnings she had given her, went unnoticed as she heard the dial tone. "The first place a criminal looks and that's where Marianne leaves the key."

A warm feeling filled Carlyn's heart as she thought of her brother and sister-in-law. Despite the personality differences, their love was secure. Bob was quiet, serious, and totally involved in top-secret computer technology for the government. Marianne, happy and talkative, adored him. Together they were devoted parents to thirteen-month-old Betsy and five-year-old Billy.

After the cleaning supplies were put away, Carlyn packed her suitcase in the neat, methodical order that was typical of all her actions. She smiled with apprehension at the plunging neckline of her black swimsuit before adding skimpy nylon bras and panties in soft pastel colors. A sheer nightie and a pure-silk negligee followed, with shorts, jeans, and two of her favorite dresses for evening wear. Her love of sensuous underclothes of delicate materials was a surprising contrast to her strong moral attitude.

Carlyn left her suitcase open and took her makeup kit into the bathroom where she stripped off her blue jeans, T-shirt, and underwear and stepped into the cool shower. Turning her back to the spray, she glided the fragrant soap over her long legs, flat abdomen, and high, full breasts. Throat arched, arms raised over her head to hold her lustrous hair, she let the water rinse the suds from her cleansed body, enjoying the feel of the cool spray against her warm skin.

Finished, she briskly dried her glistening body with a soft velour bathsheet, feeling refreshed and invigorated. She pulled up a pair of snug-fitting designer jeans in chocolate brown and fastened the waistband over a brown print silk blouse. With efficient strokes she smoothed the tumbled waves of her hair before clasping it in a chignon at the nape of her neck. A light application of mascara to naturally dark lashes, a touch of lipgloss, and a spray of rose-scented perfume to her throat and she was ready.

She fastened her suitcase after including her makeup kit and toiletries and stepped into strappy leather sandals that matched her shoulder bag, her official uniform purse with handcuffs left hanging in the back of the closet at Marianne's suggestion. Adjusting the purse strap, she took a last look around the apartment and exited, pausing to make certain her door was latched securely. The elevator took her smoothly to the basement garage where her three-year-old Volkswagen was parked.

She eased her way into the flow of traffic, driving toward the city of Santa Monica. An excellent driver, she competently maneuvered through the heavy stream of automobiles. Turning north on Highway One toward Malibu, she estimated it would take about thirty minutes to reach her destination.

Her glistening hair bound neatly on the nape of her neck emphasized the purity of her profile. Ignoring several admiring glances from passing drivers, she calmly kept pace with the flow of traffic. Without vanity about her appearance Carlyn was not aware that, in an area known the world over for its many beautiful women, she managed to stand apart with a unique, innocent loveliness.

Her unusual silvery hair glistened, contrasting sharply with naturally dark winged brows and thick lashes. Expressive eyes were large, their violet color changing from velvety purple to deep gray, depending upon her emotions. A full sensuous mouth constantly drew a man's eye. Her nose was small and straight. Taller than average, she moved gracefully, her shapely bosom and long legs giving her a regal appearance.

Rock music filled the small car when she turned on the radio, its lively sound adding to her upbeat mood. Happy, content with her life, she reflected on her long-term ambition to be a police officer, following in her father's footsteps.

Retired as a lieutenant after twenty-five years, her father, Doug, lived in southern Oregon. An avid fisherman and radio buff, he had purchased a small farm bordering the Rogue River. His hobbies kept him busy, though he missed his children and grandchildren.

Carlyn was twelve years old when her mother died, but she remembered the love and happiness she had received in abundance. Her mother had been killed by a drug-crazed youth fleeing a burglary—a needless waste that had left her family devastated and shocked. The constant love of her father and her brother's attention helped appease the grief during this traumatic period of her young life.

Quiet and studious through her teen-age years, Carlyn showed little interest in boys, despite the constant string of admirers as her figure matured and beauty began to blossom. A very strict father and protective older brother deterred even the most persistent suitor from bothering her.

After graduating from high school with advanced scholastic honors, she breezed through U.C.L.A. Her quick mind and keen intelligence easily grasped the fundamentals of her liberal-arts courses.

Well liked, with a broad circle of fascinating friends, she led a varied and interesting social life. Her basic femininity was satisfied by keeping a sparkling home and entertaining with tasty meals. She was an amateur gourmet and especially enjoyed the challenge of preparing a variety of foreign dishes.

With a college degree, eager to be self-supporting, she moved into her own apartment and immediately applied for a job on the police force. The intervening years had been exciting and full. Carlyn's energy and enthusiasm for life, her happy personality and generosity, kept her busy and content. If the thought occasionally crept into her mind that she was not fulfilled as a woman, did not have that special person to share her love with, she forced it away quickly. She refused to dwell on her intermittent desire for marriage and motherhood or her continued inability to meet a man she could eagerly share an intimate relationship with.

Stopped at a red light, she murmured beneath her breath, scolding herself for her moody introspection. "I wouldn't get married even if I found the right man. I love my job, my apartment is just the way I like it, my bank account is healthy, and all of my friends are sincere. Heart whole and fancy free, that's me! Not a depressing love affair in sight."

Toot! Toot! Varoom . . . varoom!

A quick glance in her rearview mirror reflected the sleek hood of a silver Porsche and the dark image of an impatient man revving his motor. He waited for her to drive forward, while the signal remained green.

Nervous and somewhat embarrassed, she ground the gears before pulling into the right-hand lane. She caught a quick glimpse of the driver from the corner of her eye as he passed with a rapid burst of speed.

"My gosh, it's him!" Despite his tanned features, partially hidden behind dark sunglasses, she recognized him instantly. She recalled from yesterday the thrust of his arrogant chin, the wavy black hair, and the wide shoulders. Stunned by the detail of her memory, she quickly attributed it to her police training, but she shivered instinctively, reacting unconsciously to his blatant masculinity.

His car rapidly disappearing from view, she stuck out her tongue in a childish gesture and scolded, "So, you drive a sixty-thousand-dollar custom-designed car. Big deal!"

She settled back, relaxed, and enjoyed the oceanfront drive, soon arriving at her destination: the world-famous Malibu beach colony. Beautiful homes were secluded and expensive, most costing several million dollars; owners were affluent and desirous of privacy including many well-known movie stars and television personalities. Bob's boss was the president of a national computer services company and could easily afford the area.

An elderly guard gave Carlyn clearance to pass, his admiration unnoticed as she drove through the gates. Slowly easing forward, she checked for address numbers, finding the home easily. With the VW parked securely in the narrow driveway, she climbed out, inhaling the strong salty smell of the ocean before reaching for her case. She looked around, eyes sparkling with excitement, awed by the visible wealth invested in the unique homes.

Heavy wrought-iron gates swung easily to expose a delightful enclosed garden. Planters and tubs overflowed with pungent orange nasturtiums or bright red velvety geraniums. Numerous ferns sprawled in disarray, hugging the shaded edge of the house. The sun shone in a clear sky, its rays bringing warmth into the private patio in a burst of golden light.

Broad hand-carved entrance doors beckoned as Carlyn stared with wonder at the luxury of the home. With her suitcase in one hand, she opened the front door, silently contemplating the breathtaking beauty of sunlight streaming through stained glass onto a profusion of plants. Beamed cathedral ceilings, glass walls, deep beige carpeting, mammoth velour couches and chairs, fireplace, book-shelves, tables, were all welcoming despite their elegance.

A quick survey took her through the bright modern kitchen and formal dining room on the second level before she ascended the short flight of stairs to the third-floor bedrooms.

Feet sinking into deep-pile white carpeting, Carlyn entered the master bedroom suite. She set her case on the floor and walked forward, running her sensitive fingers over the smooth surface of the pecan contemporary dresser. An aqua velvet spread and floor-length drapes, pulled to the side of a full wall of glass, looked theatrical though harmonious with original art and priceless antiques. The final effect was dramatic and luxurious.

Carlyn opened and stepped through the glass doors onto a smaller deck overlooking the seaward side of the house. She inhaled the pungent sea air, stretching her arms wide, wishing it were possible to embrace the beauty of the view, feeling delighted with Marianne's phone call and unexpected offer. Her eyes lingered on the waves surging restlessly across the sandy shore.

Eager to feel the sun on her body, she returned to the bedroom and removed her jeans and blouse quickly. Brief wisps of underwear were discarded before tugging a black swimsuit upward over the graceful curve of shapely feminine hips. Appalled to see how high the sides were cut, she felt more naked than when she wore bra and panties. Completely backless, with a plunging neckline, it was held together by thin laces tied a few inches above her waist.

Carlyn had never before worn the suit, which was a birthday gift from Marianne. She realized now it was another attempt by her sister-in-law to shatter any prudish inhibitions. Tying the narrow halter straps around the back of her neck, she entered the bathroom to inspect her image in the mirror.

The lavish bathroom, with sunken marble tub, oval

23

sinks, and gold-streaked wall mirrors, was elegantly feminine. Carlyn tugged on her suit in a vain attempt to cover the excessive amount of exposed creamy breast. Vivid against the thin black nylon material, her image was startling sensual.

Unpinned, her thick hair cascaded down her back to hang in silken waves, shimmering platinum in the bathroom light. She stood looking at her figure critically. Its curvaceous perfection failed to impress her as she determined she was much too pale and reached for a large bathsheet before leaving the room.

Thick carpeting muffled all sound as Carlyn descended the stairs, deciding to start on her suntan immediately. The partially sheltered overhang of the lower deck would be an ideal place. The sun's rays wouldn't be so apt to burn in the diffused light.

Wide sliding glass doors slid smoothly aside as she stepped outdoors. Warmth from the smooth redwood deck felt good against the soles of her bare feet while she pulled the lounge into the sunlight. The large bathsheet covered the lounge mattress completely and would be more comfortable, she thought, bending to smooth out a crease in the fluffy material.

Stretched full length on her stomach, she rested, face turned sideways on her forearm. Long minutes passed, the sunlight soaking into her body, warming her cream-colored skin with a velvety caress. Tensions from her demanding job abated quickly with the muffled sound of the ocean to soothe her senses.

Drowsy and content, Carlyn dozed, not hearing the man's footsteps bounding up the deck stairs from the beach below. Nor was she aware of his low gasp when he caught sight of her stunning figure.

CHAPTER TWO

Silent, he crossed the deck, staring at Carlyn peacefully resting on the padded lounge. His broad shoulders and powerful body towered over her slender figure as she slept. Dark lashes hooded the expression in his charcoal-gray eyes. A surge of desire filled his loins as he stared at her lustrous wavy hair, the satiny texture of her naked back, her rounded buttocks clad in the skintight black swimsuit, and the length of her shapely legs.

Roused by the enigmatic glance of the stranger, Carlyn opened her eyes. She felt a frisson of excitement as she recognized him but, startled by his unexpected appearance, gave a soft cry before quickly rising to a sitting position. He stood motionless at her side, his gaze aloof and forbidding.

"Who are you? What do you want?" she questioned in a breathless voice, her hand placed protectively over the deep-cut neckline of her swimsuit. Stunned by his size, the ease with which he confronted her, she remained seated. Disbelief filled her mind.

"One question at a time, please," he drawled, his deep, vibrant voice sending a quiver down her spine. "I'm your neighbor, Nick Sandini. What I want, that I dare tell you, is the use of your phone. Mine is out of order and I'm expecting a business call." Hands resting on his narrow hips, he watched her, his eyes drawn to the thin laces covering the enticement of the deep shadowy cleavage between her firm breasts.

Inhaling nervously, Carlyn lowered her lashes, her limbs starting to tremble beneath the searing message visible in his eyes. There was a silent communication of sexual interest more potent than anything she had dreamed possible on first contact. He was the dark, arrogant man she had seen while talking to Sergeant Broderick, the man whose image she had recalled so clearly, the person who had rudely tooted at her to get out of his way, the owner of the expensive Porsche. Without exception Nick Sandini was the most virile-appearing, dynamic-looking man she had ever met.

At a disadvantage sitting on the edge of the lounge, she started to rise. Nick reached out his right hand and helped her to her feet. As their fingers touched, Carlyn felt a nervous tremor run up her arm, causing her heart to pound erratically and her legs to feel strangely weak.

She felt dwarfed by his size. He easily topped her five-foot-eight-inch height by seven or eight inches. Her eyes never wavered from him, his description searing a permanent imprint on her mind. Trained to be observant, she didn't miss a detail of importance: approximately thirty-six, two hundred twenty pounds of taut muscle, wavy black hair growing low on his neck, piercing dark gray eyes, tanned complexion, powerful build, and fit.

The black cashmere sweater and casual slacks were obviously tailored to his size, outlining each sinewy muscle. His nose was straight and arrogant, set beneath eyes glinting with a look of controlled fire, lashes thick and straight. He was a totally masculine man, with a sensual mouth and firm chin. His stance exuded awareness, seductive expertise, and knowledge of a woman's innermost needs.

Marianne will never believe it, Carlyn thought. *I'm in Malibu for only two hours and I'm already making contact with a tall, dark, and handsome man.* Lashes lowered, Carlyn flushed faintly as she pictured his broad chest beneath the sweater, knowing instinctively it would be covered with a mat of dark hair.

His well-shaped hand still clasping her fingers, he pulled her closer, staring intently at her left hand. With reluctance she inhaled the clean male odor of his body, his warmth reaching out to enfold her. Overwhelmed, she jerked free of his hold, as if on fire, scorched by the look in his smoldering eyes.

"You're more beautiful than I imagined," he whispered hoarsely.

"You—you recognized me?"

"Immediately! You look even more delectable with your silvery hair trailing down your back." Nick's husky voice lowered intimately as he scanned her figure without embarrassment. "I see no wedding or engagement ring. Are you available?"

"For what?"

"Me."

Eyes sparkling deep violet, she glared at him, unsettled by the serious tone of his audacious comment. "I'm not available for any man. The phone's on the end table next to the couch," she retorted, pointing to the living room.

He stood motionless, his gaze aware of the sudden tautening of her breasts skimpily covered in the thin material of her swimsuit, and whispered softly, "Ah, but I'm not just any man."

With a brief "Excuse me," Carlyn fled up the stairway to the bedroom, as he started toward the telephone. Heart beating rapidly, she pulled on the matching beach jacket. It barely reached the bottom of her hips and it emphasized the smooth skin of her rounded thighs, but the front ties at least gave a modicum of modesty by veiling the excessive amount of cleavage. His searing look had been as potent as she imagined a caress with the tips of his long fingers would be—a thought that brought a sudden flush to her face.

Forcing herself to walk slowly down the stairs, Carlyn blamed her unsettled emotions on the conversation with her sister-in-law. She compelled herself to set her shoulders straight and relax before entering the living room.

Nick was hanging up the phone when she entered, a smile tugging the corners of his mouth on noticing her beach jacket. His teeth were white against his tanned face, his words teasing sardonically. "It wasn't necessary to cover up your magnificent figure. I certainly haven't reached the age when I can't remember each curve of your body. In addition that piece of lace you think is securely covering you only entices me with seductive glimpses of your skin."

Rigid, she controlled the urge to berate him severely for his boldness. She clasped her hands tightly at her sides and bit back an angry retort, instead saying calmly, "Please leave, Mr. Sandini, now that you have completed your call."

Laughing at her obvious agitation, he quipped, "I can't, Miss Thomas."

"You know my name?" Embarrassed, she realized he had overheard Sergeant Broderick's suggestive teasing. "Why can't you leave?" she demanded, uncomfortable at the intimacy of his lingering glances.

"I can't leave until I thank you for the use of the phone." One eyebrow raised in query, he continued. "And, yes, I do know your name. That officer propositioning you had a loud, clear voice. I also heard you tell him no in no uncertain terms. But what is your first name?"

"Carlyn. Now leave!"

He smiled broadly, watching with pleasure the velvety glints in her sparkling eyes and the faint tilt of her narrow chin. Undaunted by her haughty reply and belligerent stance, he walked forward, took her hand in his broad palm, and held it firmly. "I'll leave but I want you to have dinner with me tonight. We'll have lasagna and salad at seven."

With nerves taut, every intention of telling him to get lost, she murmured, "Yes." Surprise struck her, but she refused to admit she was eagerly looking forward to his company and was quivering with excitement at the thought of learning more about him.

"A woman of few words, I see." His hands reached for her shoulders and he drew her forward, their bodies lightly touching. His head descended, his mouth brushed delicately against her forehead, his warm breath disturbed the silken strands of her hair as he whispered, "Until seven . . . *buon giorno, mi amore.*"

The featherlight touch of his lips, the intensity of his hard male mouth, and the potent smell of his musky aftershave made her stomach muscles tremble, excitement running over her heated skin. She drew back in alarm at her own response.

Satisfied by her reaction, he smiled as he released her hand before turning to leave. Lithe strides carried him quickly through the open glass doors, onto the deck, and down the stairs, out of sight.

As she stood there trembling for several moments, Carlyn wondered at the tumultuous effect of Nick's presence. He was certainly not the first handsome man to touch her, she admitted, but he was the first man she had wanted to touch in return. Her hands had ached to stroke the breadth of his shoulders, his firm chin, the black hair curling at the nape of his neck, his sensuous mouth.

Dismayed by her unaccustomed sensual longing, she fled to the bedroom and impatiently pulled her swimsuit from her heated body. She dressed in white shorts and a violet T-shirt, then fled down the stairs, her bare feet hardly touching the thick carpet.

She scrambled over the soft sand to the edge of the tide, where the dampness made the footing firm, and she stood, legs braced, looking at the beauty of the Pacific Ocean, as the waves broke far out, the lacy foam a white ruffle on the deep blue sea. The breeze lifted and caressed her long hair, blowing it away from her face.

Carlyn began to race along the shoreline, her hair streaming in silky strands behind her, her long legs flashing, her bare feet skimming the gritty sand in a burst of exuberance. Soft squeals of delight were heard as she splashed through the cold water of a wave breaking close to shore.

Sea gulls screeched their disapproval at being disturbed, becoming airborne in a flush, their white bodies and silver-tipped wings outlined against the sky. After several hundred feet Carlyn strolled quietly, regaining her breath while searching for shells and other treasures of the sea. She deliberately dawdled but arrived back in time to prepare leisurely for her date with Nick.

Undressed, Carlyn entered the luxurious bathroom. Brass spigots in the shape of swans added to the elegance of the marble tub. She poured a generous portion of scented bubble bath in the warm water, then lay back, her head resting against the tub edge, silvery strands of damp curls framing her heart-shaped face.

The sound of Nick's name echoed in the room as Carlyn repeated it softly over and over. She enjoyed the way it rolled off her tongue, short and concise.

Finished, she stood, drying her glistening limbs with the soft towel before sprinkling powder in a cloud of flowery scent around her naked shoulders. With the towel wrapped sarong-fashion around her body she sat before the mirror, experimenting with hairdos and makeup until completely satisfied.

As she reentered the bedroom she saw the outfit she had chosen laid out on her bed, and wondered whether it was appropriate, but she had packed such a limited wardrobe that she knew it would have to do. She dressed in tiny bikini panties and a matching bra of lavender silk with ivory lace appliqués. They clung to her body like a second skin. The bright plum crepe dress she let fall over her shoulders was soft, its shirred skirt swirling gracefully around her shapely limbs, its high neckline discreetly buttoned with tiny pearls. A half-dozen silver bracelets jangled on the full-length cuffed sleeves as she fastened the straps of dainty evening sandals.

Satisfied with her reflection in the full-length mirror, she dabbed perfume on her throat and wrists, then walked out onto the deck outside the master bedroom. The tangy dampness of the salt-filled air drifted in from the ocean. Her mind in turmoil with thoughts of Nick, she tried to relax by watching the waves ripple along the shoreline and by listening to the delightful cry of the sea gulls as they flew over the tranquil sea.

Her revelry was interrupted by the sound of the front-door chimes. She caught her breath and tried to calm herself as she descended the stairs. Chin tilted in an attempt to appear disinterested, she opened the door. Nick stood nonchalantly before her, dressed in a gray silk shirt, black narrow slacks, and gray loafers. He looked devastatingly handsome and totally at ease.

"Miss me?" he asked mischievously, cupping her shoulders in his broad palms. "Let me look at you." His eyes seemed to penetrate her very being, and his nostrils flared at the heady fragrance of her scented skin. "You're more gorgeous each time I see you."

Carlyn's lashes fluttered nervously before she found her gaze locked with Nick's, his eyes narrowed, his look intense. Silent, they stared, their thoughts reaching out to each other in a moment filled with the tension of awareness.

Nick shook her lightly, his voice husky. "Don't look at me like that—I came here to take you to dinner not to bed! I'm delighted you're ready; your appearance has whetted my appetite." Her shoulders trembled unconsciously before he dropped his hands.

Guided by his firm palm in the small of her back, she picked up a wispy hand-crocheted stole and small silver purse, desperate to quell her rising awareness of his sensuality.

They crossed the patio, walking side by side toward the house next door. She pulled back as he led her toward the stairway to his home, having expected to get into his Porsche.

"I thought we were going to dinner," she inquired warily.

"We are. At my house." Seeing her start to protest, he silenced her. "Don't waste time objecting. I'm an excellent cook and you won't have to worry about my car running out of gas on the way home." His eyes gleamed with knowledge of her indecision and he teased affectionately.

With a soft laugh she preceded him up the steps into an equally elegant home, though furnished in more masculine taste. The living room contained a small table drawn up to a tinted-glass wall with two upholstered chairs placed side by side against it.

Nick eased the stole from Carlyn's shoulders before taking her purse to place them on the back of the broad couch. She stared at the setting sun visible through the large window, unaware of Nick's return until he placed both hands on her waist and pulled her back against the curve of his hardened masculine body.

Carlyn's breath caught in her throat, tension mounting between them as Nick lowered his head to place his lips on the side of her neck in a kiss so gentle yet so intimate, she was stunned by her response. "Please, Nick, don't—don't rush me."

He agreed readily, smiling as he turned her toward him. "Excellent idea. I don't want our dinner to ruin and I have a feeling that once I kiss you I'll be lost to all else for the rest of the night."

Pleased by his consideration of her feelings, she looked around the room nervously until he returned from the kitchen, his arms holding a brass tray heaped with a taste-tempting array of food. "If it's as delicious as it smells, you must be an excellent cook," she complimented him, inhaling the spicy aroma of the steaming lasagna.

"It is and I am. Sit to the right of me, little one, and let me serve you."

As Nick served their dinner Carlyn observed with interest. Her keen appetite and curiosity about different foods added to her enjoyment as she watched. With assurance and skill that surprised her he placed antipasto on the table. Spicy peppers, black olives, thin salami slices, sharp provolone, artichoke hearts, stuffed egg halves, pickled mushrooms, radish roses, and crunchy celery.

Carlyn lifted an artichoke heart to her mouth and tasted it. "Hmm . . . olive oil, wine, basil. . . ."

"Very good, my little gourmet, but don't try to wheedle the lasagna sauce recipe from me. It's an old family secret," he teased in a husky voice. "One passed from father to son!"

Carlyn's fork slid through the wide noodles as she cut a bite. Smothered in tangy meat and tomato sauce, thick with ricotta and mozzarella cheese, and topped with pungent Parmesan, it was the best pasta she had ever eaten.

The salty sea air and her long run on the beach had given her a healthy appetite. Nick smiled fondly as he watched her eat every succulent morsel of her dinner.

The sun set in a vivid burst of fiery crimson streaks over

the horizon as Carlyn watched, uneasy with her growing intrigue in Nick. She delighted in his sharp mind and keen sense of humor, which had her chuckling easily throughout the leisurely meal.

Replete, they relaxed with glasses of dark burgundy wine. Carlyn listened intently, not surprised to find that Nick owned a well-known chain of restaurants. There had been practiced skill in the preparation and serving of their meal. He mentioned that most of his time was spent traveling between restaurants to ensure that his exacting quality requirements and standards were maintained.

When Nick queried Carlyn about her life, she changed the subject abruptly. Conscious of her evasiveness, Nick remained silent, planning to bide his time until she was more relaxed in his company. He calmly explained that his mother was an American, but his father was Italian born. They had returned to Italy a few years ago. Both had taught him early in life the necessity of working hard to accomplish his goals.

Nick's father and mother had owned a small family restaurant in San Francisco and he had grown up learning each phase of their business. With an inherent ability in management, energetic aggressiveness, and determination Nick went on to build a chain of outstanding Italian restaurants in many of the leading United States cities. At thirty-five he found himself wealthy beyond his dreams—a satisfied man, whose lucrative business and varied social life was the envy of his many friends.

Nick stood, assisting Carlyn with her chair before helping her to her feet. "Dance with me, Carlyn?" he asked, his voice husky.

So absorbed by Nick and their conversation she had paid little attention to the soft music playing in the background, but now she turned to him willingly. Hand raised to his shoulders, eager to feel his touch, she trembled.

Nick's arms circled her pliant body, drawing her to him

in a close embrace. They danced in silence to the slow music, his hold becoming more intimate as he felt her body relax. He turned his face toward her, trailing moist, sensuous kisses on her neck.

Carlyn's breath caught sharply when she felt Nick's tongue seductively touch her ear. In a tremulous motion she gripped his iron-hard shoulders. "No, Nick! Please don't. Just dance."

His steps slowed as he circled to the music's arousing tempo. Hands sliding possessively down the length of her spine, he drew her close against his tautened contours. Deliberately he teased, his seeking mouth moving provocatively, intimately, along the smooth line of her jaw, the satiny skin of her face, and the corner of her pulsating lips, until she shuddered with yearning.

An ardent moan escaped Carlyn as she placed her hands on the back of Nick's head, raising on tiptoes so she could stop the taunting seduction of his lips with her soft mouth. Fingers threaded through his ebony hair, she smoothed it on his nape in a loving caress.

All pretense of playfulness gone, Nick took her face in his hands and pressed his mouth hard against her lips, his tongue probing expertly, trying to pry them apart. He was stunned to feel her pull away as his kiss deepened, her body twisting frantically to break his hold. "What's the matter, *mia cara?*" he whispered, concerned when he saw the look of quandary in her wary eyes. "Did I hurt you?"

"I've never allowed anyone to kiss me that way before, Nick," she answered truthfully, color rising in her cheeks. "It's—it's so . . . intimate."

"It's supposed to be. Come back to my arms. Let me hold you while we dance until you feel more capable of responding to me. I warned you earlier that once I touched you, I would be lost to all else!"

Once more in the comforting hold of Nick's arms, Carlyn knew it wasn't her inability to respond that stopped her, but the wild rushing of sensual pleasure she felt from his caress, shocking her with the intensity of her own awakening needs. Her breath quickened as his potent masculinity worked its spell, their steps perfectly matched while moving to the romantic beat of the music.

Nick stopped, his gaze smoldering as it locked with the dreamy look in her darkening eyes. His hands slid from the small of her back to her nape, where his fingers stroked the silken strands of her silvery hair. His dark head descended slowly, making her wait for the touch of her lips. Loins aching, he watched her eyes close in a vain attempt to conceal her mounting passion.

"You act so damn innocent and young," he murmured against her face.

"I'm twenty-five!" she retorted, her face flushed from his look.

"Twenty-five and never been properly kissed—until now!" Confident of his own skill, he stroked her lips with his tongue. His hands lowered to fondle the curve of her spine. His experienced touch arousing her body through her thin dress, he kissed her with such tender sensitivity that she parted her lips without hesitation.

There was no restraint as he probed the moist inner sweetness with his seeking tongue. The unaccustomed explosive intimacy of such a ravishing kiss awoke a fiery need in Carlyn. Moaning softly, she arched her supple body up toward him, her breasts pressed firmly against the bruising strength of his heaving chest. Her lips softened, answering the driving force of his hungry kiss with a seeking response of her own.

At Nick's touch Carlyn's mind reeled with the devastating awareness she had of him as a man. His superb control was totally unlike the advances and hurried moist kisses she had parried so adamantly in the past. With a quiver running over her sensitive skin she moved instinc-

tively, her slender hands feeling the hardness of his powerful shoulders.

Nick raised his face, reluctantly breaking contact with
the magic of Carlyn's parted lips. Sexual desires tightly
checked, he trailed gentle kisses over her closed eyelids
and satiny smooth face before resting his mouth against
the curve of her neck.

Carlyn's senses heightened from the scent of his potent
after-shave and clean male body; she raised her face, eyes
a deep violet.

"My God, Carlyn, I can't believe you! How in the hell
did you control your passionate nature all these years?
Were your partners all so inept that they couldn't kindle
the flame that burns within your beautiful body?" He
moaned huskily, pulling her head to his chest. Cradling
her gently, he let his unsteady fingers run through the
satiny strands of her glistening hair, as she refused to
answer.

Nick's harsh, throaty voice and trembling body made
Carlyn realize for the first time her power to arouse and
excite. Despite her little previous experience her response
had surged forward with fervent ardency. She received
pleasure listening to the unsteady beat of his heart, feeling
her hands circling his waist for balance, content to be
silent.

Nick expelled his breath sharply, pushing her away as
he ran his hand over the nape of his neck in consternation.
"What a contradiction you are. You respond to me physically, have a body men have surely been after for years,
yet you've never been passionately kissed before." Grabbing her arm, he commanded grimly, "We're going for a
walk on the beach. For your safety I hope to hell the ocean
breeze is cooler than my blood!"

He reached for his sport jacket and placed it around her
shoulders before ushering her gently out the door, down
the steps, and onto the sand all in one quick motion.

Carlyn walked silently by Nick's side, having difficulty keeping up with his long impatient strides. Her thoughts disturbed, she was forced to admit her hypocrisy and smugness about high morals. Tonight had shown her how wrong she was. Her heart, still pounding from his tumultuous kiss, told her she had never previously been tempted.

Nick glanced at Carlyn's downcast face, visible in the moonlight, as his hand squeezed her shoulder. "I wanted your fragrance on my jacket," he informed her, explaining his reason for not letting her wear her stole. "Now whenever I wear it, I will be reminded of our first date."

Bothered by the seriousness of his voice, she stopped and bent to remove her sandals. Holding the narrow straps in her hand, she began to race along the edge of the surf, her slender bare feet wet with foam from the ebbing tide. As Nick's jacket began to slide from her shoulders, Carlyn groped awkwardly at it and lost her balance. As she was about to fall to the sand she was caught in Nick's strong clasp.

He swung her around breathlessly and pulled her to him. As they stood there—he holding her firmly, she resting her head on his wide chest—the pounding of his heart was equal to the rhythm of her own as they embraced at the edge of the Pacific ocean.

"Why did you run from me, *cara?* Surely you know the male has strong hunting instincts and flight gives impetus to them? You didn't think you had a chance of outrunning me, did you?" he teased.

Carlyn raised her face. Looking at Nick's proud features outlined in the moonlight, she replied saucily, "Of course. If your jacket hadn't fallen off, I could have beat you easily. You'll just have to wonder now though, as I'm through running for the night!"

Nick groaned with a sudden surge of desire, exclaiming hoarsely, "You're through running, all right, and this is why!" His mouth lowered to her upturned face and he kissed each eyelid tenderly before slowly moving to her waiting lips. Beneath the pale moon his mouth took hers, branding a permanent seal of possession on her vulnerable heart.

Eager now to experience the intimacy of Nick's fiery kisses, Carlyn raised on tiptoe to meet his mouth and felt his hands spread over her lower back. She trembled beneath the touch of his hard male mouth, her soft lips parting to admit his questing tongue. Legs splayed to balance her weight, she felt the intimate touch of his aroused maleness and the shocking desire to move against him. His hand reached for her fingers and placed them in the neckline of his shirt, directly over his pounding heart.

"Feel what you do to me, Carlyn? My heart has never beat so fast, nor have I felt so aroused. You have totally bewitched me tonight."

Carlyn rubbed her fingertips across the thick mat of hair on Nick's heaving chest. Entranced, she reveled in her first intimate touch of a man's body, eager to explore his well-defined muscles and absorb their exciting warmth.

Nick pulled her closer and moaned her name, then bent her backward with the force of his firm mouth crushing her lips in a bruising kiss. His hand slid to her bodice, cupped her breast briefly. Abruptly he pushed her away, standing for a moment with his back to her before turning to put his jacket around her shoulders. Hand in hand they walked toward her home.

Nick shortened his long stride to match Carlyn's as they made their way silently across the damp sand. The deserted beach was rapidly cooling, a light fog beginning to creep in. Silvery foam swept over the sand, coming close to their feet, as they strolled unaware, each deep in his own thoughts.

Nearing her home, Nick stopped to turn her gently in his arms, his lips brushing her forehead in a brief kiss. "I hope you realize I didn't want to stop, Carlyn. My greatest desire was to lower you to the sand and continue making love. From your response I don't think you would have denied me. Am I right?"

Head raised proudly, eyes shimmering with unshed tears, Carlyn shook her head, feeling he had rejected her. In a voice trembling with disappointment she retorted, "No! I place a high price on my love, Nick, and you most certainly could not have taken me on a sandy beach."

"Little liar!" He laughed huskily. "Do you think a man doesn't know when a woman is willing to make love? You may have a high price, my dear, but I don't think you would have taken time to bargain had I started to make love to you in earnest—not just those few innocent kisses and nibbles you've received so far."

"Innocent!" She flushed thinking that there was nothing innocent about the man or his experienced sexual technique. She refused to comment on his blunt remark, watching surreptitiously as he escorted her through the gate, opened the front door, and checked to ensure the home was safe for her to enter.

The golden glow of the porch light outlined his towering form as he looked at her. His eyes held her, expression carefully veiled, as he raised her chin. She felt his thumb outline her lips, his searing touch already familiar, her reaction coming unbidden.

"Sweet dreams, *mia cara.*" His voice, barely above a low whisper, fanned her face, his breath was as clean as his person, his kiss brief.

Carlyn watched speechless as Nick left, heard the sound of the door closing, but stood motionless, her mind whirling with the traumatic turn of events. Touching her sensitive lips, she cried in a plaintive voice, "Dear God, please don't let him be married."

She walked slowly up the stairs to the master bedroom and undressed automatically, deep in thought. Clad in a sheer lavender nightgown, she slipped between cool satin sheets, luxuriously stretching her legs on the soft mattress.

She gradually drifted into a deep, contented sleep, Nick foremost in her thoughts, her last knowledge a silent prayer that he was free to care.

CHAPTER THREE

Gray fog lay like a heavy damp blanket against the bedroom window as Carlyn awoke early the next morning. She stepped outside and walked barefoot to the edge of the deck. Slim legs visible below the thigh-length gown, she yawned sleepily, her silver hair a mass of tumbled curls from her night's sleep.

As she peered through the fog she noticed a lone figure jogging at the edge of the surf. Her heart increased its beat when she recognized Nick. Barefoot, wearing navy-blue jogging pants with a white stripe down the sides of the legs and a matching loose sweat shirt, he ran effortlessly over the sand with long graceful strides.

Carlyn leaned on the railing, impulsively yelling, "Nick! How would you like me to make your breakfast? You're not the only cook in the world, you know!"

Nick stopped, legs apart, hands resting on his narrow hips, damp black hair matted around his forehead. As he looked up, one dark brow raised, he exclaimed huskily, "Good morning, Juliet. If you don't want me to play Romeo, you better leave the balcony and get dressed!" Laughing as she quickly pulled back in embarrassment, he continued. "That bit of lavender lace is much too enticing at this hour of the morning, especially with me all sweaty from my run along the beach. Give me twenty minutes and I'll see how well you cook, but I warn you I've yet to meet a woman who can prepare a meal to my satisfaction."

"Chauvinist!"

"You bet. Now get moving. If I find you wearing that sexy nightie when I return, I guarantee neither of us will eat breakfast. Probably miss lunch and dinner as well," he teased boldly.

Flushing deeper at his suggestive comments, Carlyn returned to the bedroom. She dressed quickly, normally deft fingers fumbling in their haste. She added a dab of pink lipstick before tying back her gleaming hair with a bright violet scarf, its ends hanging over her shoulders for a touch of color.

As she checked through the groceries that Bob and Marianne had left, she planned her menu. Arms filled, she closed the door of the wide double-door refrigerator with her hip, intent on trying to impress Nick with her culinary skills. Within minutes bacon was sizzling on the stove, coffee was perking, eggs were waiting to be fried, and bread was in the toaster ready for the handle to be pushed down.

She took a chilled pineapple from the crisper, then sliced it in quarters on the counter. Juicy chunks resting on the thick skin, a bright maraschino cherry speared with a toothpick sitting in the center of each serving, it made a delicious addition to their menu.

The aroma of sizzling bacon filled the room while she set the table with attractive china on woven place mats. Bacon draining on a paper towel, she cracked three eggs into a small pan. Butter bubbled around the edge as they slowly cooked. Pushing the toaster handle down on four thin slices of whole-wheat bread, she took a quick glance at the clock.

Nick's knocking was timed perfectly. She let him in, then exclaimed over her shoulder as she ran back to the kitchen, "Hurry up or your egg yolks will be hard, and thanks for returning my stole and purse."

With swift, competent hands she poured coffee, buttered toast, slid perfectly cooked eggs onto their plates, and added crisp bacon strips, waiting expectantly for his comments.

Nick pulled out Carlyn's chair before seating himself opposite her. "I'm truly amazed to find a woman who cooks bacon crisp, doesn't break egg yolks, and butters toast while it's still hot," he said, enjoying the smells rising from the table. "This looks like ambrosia to me after a four-mile jog on the beach. If the coffee is strong enough, I'll put you under lock and key forever." A smile tugged at Carlyn's lips at his teasing.

Each mouthful was so delicious, it was a few moments before he noticed Carlyn had not touched her breakfast. Nick took her hand, held it firmly, his thumb moving in a sensuous caress across her palm. "What's the matter, honey?"

"Are you married, Nick?" she blurted out, expression distressed.

"Does it matter?" he whispered huskily, dark eyes holding her gaze while he waited for an answer.

Carlyn lowered her eyes in an attempt to break the intensity of Nick's look. "Of course it does. I only fraternize with married men during my working hours."

"Then feel free to fraternize to your heart's content. I'm not married nor have I ever desired to be." After taking a satisfying drink of hot coffee, he set the cup in the saucer before adding casually, "To be frank, I've always had more than my share of women."

As her fingers trembled in his clasp a grave look clouded

his expression. "Surely you didn't think I was a thirty-five-year-old virgin?" he inquired earnestly. "I never had any inclination to study for the priesthood nor have I dated women who desired to be nuns!" Releasing her hand, he scolded softly, "Eat your breakfast before it gets cold. I'll put the dishes in the washer, then I have business to take care of the rest of the day."

Carlyn sat motionless, filled with jealousy, trying to block from her mind the image of Nick making love to other women. To her dismay she found her first passion brought with it a bout of red-hot possessive resentment.

Reading her features correctly, Nick commanded, "Look at me, *cara!*"

Obediently she raised her face, flushing as she felt tension mount between them.

"Don't think about it, sweetheart. They were my past. You and you alone are my future." Watching her push her plate aside, he chided gently, "Eat your breakfast like a good girl. I have to be in Los Angeles by nine and I want to finish this excellent meal without the distraction of sudden censorship of my wicked past." Rising, he emptied his coffee cup in one long swallow before reaching for his plate to clear the table.

"Leave the dishes, Nick," Carlyn stated coolly. "If you're in a hurry, that's fine with me. And there's no need to hurry back on my account. Until yesterday I managed quite well by myself!"

"Okay, crosspatch," he teased. "Thanks for the meal. Someday I may even take you in hand and teach you to cook." After glancing at his watch, he grabbed her shoulders and pulled her from the chair. As he held her against the firm muscles of his body, he jerked the scarf from her hair with amazing speed.

"Ouch! That hurt, you . . . big brute." She stormed with fury, struggling, futilely, to free herself from his arms.

"Then I shall kiss it better." Immediately he lowered his

mouth to cover her indignant lips. Passion flared instantly as his hold tightened. Cupping her face, he inhaled the fragrance of her skin, his tongue slowly outlining the shape of her lips, their breath intermingling. He shuddered with the feel of her supple body curving to his.

Carlyn was unable to stop the sudden response of her traitorous body, her breasts swelling beneath the pressure of his broad chest. It was as if his mouth had never left her lips from the night before. Her senses were inflamed with insatiable hunger, as his kiss continued with rising desire.

His hands slid intimately down her narrow rib cage, hesitated to cup the mature roundness of both breasts, then resumed their exploration of her slender waist and her hips. Grasping their curves, he pulled her inexorably closer, his own body balancing her graceful form. When his kiss ended, he noticed tears spilling from her eyes. Against his will he removed his hands, stepping away from the havoc he had unwittingly created on her awakening emotions with the expertise of his experienced touch.

"God, sweetheart, don't cry. This was only supposed to be a quick good-bye kiss, not a permanent farewell."

With his handkerchief he gently wiped her tears and placed a tender kiss in their place. "I'm sorry, little one. I should have remembered from last night how volatile caressing you can be. Forgive me?" Cradling her face to his chest, stroking her tumbled hair, he soothed her with soft crooning whispers against her ear. "Carlyn, you don't need cooking lessons—or kissing lessons—but as good as breakfast tasted, your mouth was far better." He released her and walked reluctantly to the door, calling over his shoulder, *"Arriverderci, mi amore."*

Carlyn stood, too emotional to utter a single word. The sound of the door closing was followed within moments by the Porsche motor as Nick left for Los Angeles. Thoughts troubled, she was uncertain how to handle her tumultuous feelings for Nick. Like a hurricane, he had entered her life, drawing her into the eye of the storm with the power of his potent masculinity. She felt wary and confused, vulnerable to the pull of his strong personality. Sensing his inherent honesty and integrity, she knew he would be baffled by her evasiveness about her past life.

Deep in thought, she returned to the kitchen to clean the breakfast things. She made up her mind to assert her strong inner resources and enjoy the remaining days of her vacation. She would enjoy each moment with Nick to the fullest. Suddenly she realized that Marianne was right: she had been living in an emotional vacuum—a vacuum that shattered at the first impact of Nick's fiery glance in West Los Angeles.

Carlyn changed into shorts and a strapless top, eager to explore the beach. Convinced she was more interested in acquiring a tan than thinking of Nick, she tried unsuccessfully to erase him from her mind.

A pleasant morning was spent walking along the shore, searching for shells. Talking with a retired couple and walking their rambunctious poodle helped pass another hour. She watched enraptured as three young boys put the finishing touches on a giant sand castle, but her soft heart sympathized when a wave washed away hours of work in one surge. Several young surfers approached, attracted by her flawless beauty, only to be given the cold shoulder. Unconsciously comparing them with Nick, she found them lacking in every way.

In the afternoon she drove to the local supermarket to shop for the ingredients of her most requested party entrée. As she unlocked her front door, arms laden with two large grocery sacks, she heard the last ring of the phone. Disappointed, she put the food away, knowing instinctively she had missed a call from Nick.

She refused to leave the house, just in case Nick phoned again, and spent the remainder of the afternoon reading the same pages of a popular best seller over and over, unable to concentrate. Bathed and dressed, she had just turned on the evening news when the phone rang. Breathless, she picked up the receiver, heart beating wildly when he greeted her.

"Honey, it's Nick. I tried to phone you around noon to let you know I won't be home until after your bedtime. I'm too busy to even talk to you now, but I had to tell you I've missed you like hell. Did you have a nice day?"

His deep voice sending a thrill along her spine, she forced herself to answer casually. "Absolutely fantastic. Each minute has been packed with excitement. I'm going to a movie now. Since you're in a hurry, I'll say good-bye." Abruptly she ended his call.

After hanging up the phone, she reached for the *TV Guide* to see if there was a movie showing. Her lie didn't seem quite so bad that way. Her stomach growled with hunger, so she fixed a sandwich, carried it to the front room, and settled on the broad couch. The early movie was as tasteless to her as the sandwich, her discontent caused by Nick's absence.

Turning her lights out at midnight, she sat in the faint moonlight, waiting restlessly for the sound of Nick's Porsche. Hours later, when he arrived, she walked to her bedroom and automatically prepared to retire. Knowing Nick had arrived home safely made Carlyn surprisingly content, and she quickly drifted off to sleep.

A heavy pounding on the front door and the insistent ringing of loud chimes woke her from deep slumber. Fumbling into her robe, she walked sleepily down the stairs. As she held her tumbled hair out of her eyes, she opened the door and peeked warily around the edge.

"Nick! What are you doing here at this hour?"

"Two things. One, seeing how you look first thing in the morning without all that war paint on, and two, bringing you your breakfast." Holding small boxes of cereal, a quart of milk, two bowls and glasses, and a pint of orange juice, he pushed his way in.

She looked at him, aware of her thin covering. "But—but—"

"No 'buts,' my love. We'll eat breakfast like any normal couple, then I'll give you a kiss on the forehead and go off to work." He walked to the kitchen, placed the breakfast things on the table, pulled out a chair, and pushed Carlyn into it.

She watched, amused, as Nick set two bowls in front of them and poured two glasses of orange juice. There was a selection of Raisin Bran, Corn Flakes, and Rice Krispies. Nonchalantly he made her choice for her, filled their bowls with cereal, poured on the milk, and started eating.

"Come on, sweetheart. You have to eat before they lose their snap, krackle, and pop." Face raised, his eyes lingered on her tenderly. "You're gorgeous without any makeup, your face flushed with sleep. I even detect the beginning of a faint tan."

Her violet eyes darkened before Carlyn blurted impulsively, "I never wear all that much makeup, or 'war paint,' as you call it, Nick. Furthermore I feel like a darn fool sitting here without my hair brushed, barely dressed, and you wearing a custom-tailored three-piece suit, groomed like a model!"

Laughing at her discomfort, he assured her she was beautiful, told her about his busy day, inquired about hers, finished his cereal, kissed her on the forehead, and left—all within fifteen minutes.

In a daze at his unexpected behavior Carlyn finished her breakfast, her heart beating with the excitement of knowing he would return around one o'clock and they would have the afternoon together. Her eyes shone as she remembered his final words: "Bake me something with chocolate in it and be in your black swimsuit when I return."

Despite his seemingly ridiculous demand, Carlyn could

hardly wait to do as he asked. In an hour she had straightened the kitchen and bedroom, dressed, shopped, and returned home.

Her father and brother were chocolate lovers and she had experimented in the kitchen many times before until satisfied that her recipe was perfect. Moist and chewy, crammed full of chocolate chips, topped with rich creamy fudge frosting, her brownies would satisfy the most discriminating chocoholic.

Determined to show Nick her talents, she set to work. In a large bowl she mixed the thick dark batter, nibbling on some of the chips, then scraped the bowl's gooey contents into a baking pan. The pleasant smell of baking wafted through the kitchen as she removed the pan from the oven a half hour later. Her own thick fudge butter frosting ready, she iced the brownies while they were still warm. She licked the frosting from the broad spatula after swirling it decoratively on the brownies, and set the pan in the middle of the kitchen table.

The tantalizing taste of chocolate still on her tongue, she murmured with self-satisfaction, "These, my arrogant friend, will absolutely melt in your mouth when you sink your pearly white teeth into their rich goodness."

The ocean air felt cool and refreshing as Carlyn walked out onto the lower deck. Far down the beach an elderly couple strolled slowly, their two dogs scampering in and out of the water. Gulls scattered, screeching angrily for being disturbed from their endless search for food. Smaller speckled white terns, with narrow bills and straight legs, marched like tiny wooden soldiers rapidly in and out of the foam at the surf's edge.

Farther down the beach young boys in wet suits were paddling their surfboards beyond the breakers, hoping to ride the crest of waves into the shore. Carlyn marveled at their perseverance. Agile and energetic, they would practice their sport from sunup to sundown.

Carlyn turned from the rail, entering the house in a sudden decision to shampoo her hair. Cleansed, a heady fragrance from the perfumed soap clinging to her skin, she stepped from the shower. She rubbed her hair briskly and wrapped it in a bathtowel before entering the bedroom to dress.

The skimpy black swimsuit that hugged her curves so sensually caused her mind to think back to the first time she actually met Nick. She recalled the fire in his eyes, the intensity of his gaze, and she hesitated, feeling suddenly shy. She tossed the matching beach jacket over her shoulders, before returning to the lower deck.

She brushed her shoulder-length hair free of tangles and fluffed it with her fingertips, then reclined on the chaise longue, content to let the midday sun dry her waves as she anticipated Nick's return.

CHAPTER FOUR

She was caught unawares as Nick bounded barefoot up the stairs, clad in a tight black bathing suit. Her lingering glance took in his powerful physique, the wide shoulders, steel-hard arms, and broad chest. A thick mat of black hair stretched across his upper torso before veeing sensually to his flat abdomen. His brief suit rode low on his narrow hips, drawing attention to his masculine virility.

Straight and sturdy, he looked like a Greek statue standing before her. Her nerves tightened alarmingly as she continued to admire the tanned beauty of his masculine body.

Realizing how intently she had been staring, she raised her eyes, her face flushing when she met his questioning look.

He helped her to her feet and pulled her into the living room. Hands possessively on her shoulders, he held her away, enabling him to return her lingering look. "Visions of you waiting for me dressed in this black piece of nothing drove all thoughts of work from my mind. I've missed you, sweetheart," he murmured, his endearment causing her heart to pound erratically. "Think you still remember what I taught you?"

"What did you teach me?" she questioned suspiciously, twisting away from his grip.

"How to kiss!" He watched with amusement as her eyes flashed fire and her hands came up to her hips defiantly.

"Why, you conceited, egotistical, chauvinistic clout! You didn't teach me a darn thing, Mr. Sandini."

Nick reached out for her and let his palms gently caress her slender waist. "Oh, yes, I did, Miss Thomas, but apparently you need a refresher course. Besides, you need to be disciplined for calling me a clout!"

She tightened her mouth into a straight line in defiance. Struggling to fight back the urge to surrender to him, she stood her ground.

Nick cupped the back of her head with one hand and raised her chin with the other, then trailed his finger lightly over her face. Slowly tracing its contours, he touched the tip of her nose and her chin and outlined the shape of her mouth, all the time staring into her widening eyes, watching the irises darken to deep purple velvet.

Her lips trembled and softened as he delicately pried them apart before moving to the arch of her slender throat. His finger rested momentarily on the rapidly beating pulse, then lowered, moving between the ties on her jacket and burning a path along the edge of her swimsuit. His knuckles pressed intimately into her soft breasts as he removed her jacket.

Knowing she had lost the fight, she allowed small groans of pleasure to escape from her throat and arched her body against him, her lips parting seductively, her eyes pleading. She felt unconcerned about the lacy covering that lay crumpled at her feet.

"Now that's better," he murmured against her mouth. Her lips, sensitized by his tormenting touch, throbbed to life as he drank endlessly of their moisture, her body responding fully to his experienced technique of seduction and deep, probing kisses.

Tormented by the passion he was able to arouse, she leaned weakly against him. Their bare legs entwined, her full breasts were crushed to his muscular chest. The brevity of their attire, combined with the feel of his steel-hard naked shoulders beneath her fingers, was too much for Carlyn.

She whimpered softly and her body shook as he continued to take his fill of her parted lips, his tongue seeking hers relentlesly. Feeling her distress, he raised his head and pressed her heated face into his chest. With a gentle touch he stroked her silky hair, letting her calm down slowly from his sensual onslaught. "Oh, Carlyn, you didn't forget one damn thing."

Burying his face into her hair, he breathed deeply of its scent, both hands slowly rubbing her back. When her heartbeat slowed, he pushed her an arm's length away. His own heart thumped uncontrollably as he saw two small tears overflow and run down her smooth cheeks. With the tip of his tongue he licked them away, pressing a tender kiss to the end of her nose before releasing her from his clasp. The beauty of the passion that filled her eyes was haunting.

Aware of her vulnerability to Nick as to no one before, Carlyn turned away. She placed her hands over her lowered face in a desperate attempt to control her heightened emotions.

In a burst of unleashed passion Nick drew her to him. Bringing his hands along her sides, he sought and found her breasts, caressed them gently and intimately. As he felt her nipples harden with desire through the thin cloth of her swimsuit, his thumbs slowly circled the tips and his fingers embraced her voluptuous curves without restraint.

Head bent, he moved her glistening hair from her shoulders with his mouth. With warm, firm lips he placed a reverent kiss on her tender nape. Reluctantly leaving the tantalizing fullness, his hands slid to her abdomen. His fingers splayed over her quivering stomach and their bodies were molded together until her sudden twisting motion was more than he could bear and he released her.

Carlyn turned to see Nick walk to the fireplace mantel, obviously disturbed by their passionate embrace. Over his shoulder he stared, dark eyes smoldering with strong passion. "Keep away, Carlyn," he commanded harshly. "I have to cool off. It was absolutely insane for me to kiss you in the privacy of the living room with us dressed so scantily. I've never doubted my self-control before, but holding you, I came near to losing it."

Nick's poignant appeal stunned her, made her aware she wasn't the only one affected by their unrestrained lovemaking.

"Tell me about your day," he asked huskily. "Talk to me, sweetheart, while I count these damn bricks on the fireplace wall. Maybe that will take my mind off the sight and feel of your body." Sculpted shoulder muscles rippled with each deep breath as Nick looked away.

"I—I made you some brownies," she stuttered. "Would you like to try one now?"

With effort Nick controlled his heightened senses enough to turn to her. "That sounds wonderful, honey. Bring them out to the deck. I could use some fresh air right now."

Carlyn returned in a few moments holding a plate with two thick squares of moist brownies in one hand and a frosty glass of milk in the other. She handed them to Nick and seated herself opposite him, watching anxiously as he took the first bite.

He smacked his lips to his fingers in an exaggerated manner and smiled. "There's no beatin' chocolate eatin'."

Carlyn chuckled at Nick's sense of humor and watched him with satisfaction as he silently ate every crumb. After he drank the glass of milk, he contentedly patted his flat abdomen and rose.

"Let's go, you delectable wench. I want to see how many days it takes your creamy skin to get as tan as mine." Taking her elbow, he led her down the stairs, picking up a blanket and towel from the deck railing and flinging them over one broad shoulder they trudged through the soft sand, her small hand clasped firmly in his. Uninterested in the row of expensive homes, they had thoughts only of each other. Carlyn was continuously impressed by his many courtesies and inherent concern for her comfort, and she felt cherished and protected.

Finding a spot at the edge of the damp sand, Nick spread out the blanket before dropping his towel on it carelessly. Without warning he took Carlyn roughly in his arms and lifted her to his chest.

She screeched with surprise but Nick ignored her, as he raced into the surf with fierce threats to drop her into the icy depths, his strong limbs carrying her effortlessly.

Playfully pummeling his broad back, she pleaded loudly, "Please, Nick! Don't drop me. I just washed my hair and I don't want to get it sticky with salt."

"Scaredy cat! Admit it, you don't know how to swim," he teased, his strong arms holding her tightly to his hair-roughened chest, while the ocean swirled around his sturdy thighs. She retaliated quickly, pulling his hair.

Her mischievous chuckles turned to yelps when he lowered her sun-warmed legs without warning into the cold ocean. His sharp slap stung her bottom as he ran through the ocean and plunged headfirst into a high wave. His physical power was evident with each stroke of the Australian crawl as he swam straight out to sea.

Not daring to look away for fear of losing sight of him, she watched anxiously as his head became a dark spot beyond the waves. She walked to their blanket only when she saw him turn and swim back toward shore. She sat down, her hands clasped around her drawn-up knees, and waited for Nick, forcing her expression to look calm so that he wouldn't see her concern for his safety.

Her breath quickened when he rose from the water; her eyes were held by the perfection of his physique as he raced up the sand. Soon he loomed over her, deliberately running his hands through his wet hair so that cold drops of seawater fell on her. Her heart beat wildly as the drops trickled through the mat of hair on his chest and down to his navel. For the first time she was aware of how sensual a man's healthy body could be. She flushed and quickly lowered her lashes to hide her awakening desire.

Nick quickly dried his sinewy torso, his eyes running over her naked back and thick shiny hair. "Lie on your stomach, sweetheart, while I run to my house and get some suntan oil. I don't want your delicate skin to burn."

Carlyn eased herself comfortably into the shape of the soft sand, the afternoon sun warm on her back. When Nick returned, he knelt over her and poured a long stream of oil down the center of her spine. His long fingers smoothed the oil into her heated skin as she wiggled contentedly into a more comfortable position on the blanket.

Smacking her shapely bottom, Nick ordered her to quit. "Lie still so I can do a good job of this. I don't want you to blister or burn."

Carlyn drew a sharp breath and lay rigid, her face resting on her crossed arms as he rubbed the oil along her sides. The feel of his hands as they massaged her skin caused the familiar churning turmoil in her abdomen. She had to force herself to keep from turning on her back and pulling his hands to her breasts. His smooth strokes along their outer contours were a potent stimulus, his intimate fondling too recent.

Nick pushed her long hair aside, untying the top of her halter. He kneaded her shoulders, his thumbs rubbing more oil on her tender skin in a gentle caress. Just when she thought she couldn't bear another minute without pleading for him to kiss her, he stopped.

Speechless, she felt a trickle of warm oil on the back of each leg. She felt his calm touch rub the oil in, starting with her ankles and proceeding up the back of her legs until he reached the bottom of her swimsuit.

When he finished, he capped the bottle and lay on his back, arms crossed beneath his head. "Well, aren't you going to congratulate me?" he asked.

"Why?" she murmured, her voice muffled against her arm.

"For not taking advantage of your languorous state and your urge to have me kiss you."

She asked honestly, "How did you know my thoughts?"

"Because they were the same as my own. Rest assured, that was in my mind all the time my hands were on your satin smooth body. Now be good and shut your eyes. A nap will do us both good."

They lay close, thighs and shoulders touching. Her body was smooth and sleek, his legs and forearms had a light covering of hair except for the thick curls on his chest. Relaxing, they dozed lazily in the warm sun.

She felt the intensity of his gaze, parting her long lashes slowly to see him staring at her, his eyes dark, his expression serious.

His voice deepened as he spoke. "This is the first time we have slept together." A smile tugged the corners of his mouth as he warned her, "I guarantee it won't be the last. Turn over now. You've had enough sun on your back today."

Forgetting the untied straps of her swimsuit top, Carlyn started to roll over but instantly felt the top slip. She grabbed the ties quickly and lay flat, her face colored with embarrassment.

Nick noticed her distress and, leaning over, tied the straps competently, his voice soothing. "Feel better now?"

"Yes, thank you," she said, rolling over gracefully onto her back. As Nick reached for the oil and removed the cap, Carlyn took it from him. "I can do my front without your help, Mr. Sandini!"

"Spoil sport, Miss Thomas!" he leered mischievously. "You get the fun side. The topography is more interesting." His look sent a shiver up her spine before bringing a hot flush to her face. "What a prim lady you are. You're actually blushing. For a twenty-five-year-old contemporary feminist you seem uniquely innocent. I still can't believe I had the pleasure of giving you your first proper kiss."

"Yes, Nick . . . it's true," she whispered, eyes downcast and dark.

Steel-gray eyes filled with desire, Nick stared possessively at her flawless figure. His husky voice was like a seductive caress. "A lifetime's search could never turn up a more responsive pupil to tutor in the art of love than you, my innocent." The muscles in his biceps and shoulders rippled as he rolled onto his side and reached out his hand to touch her, his mind filled with awe that they had met.

Drawing her stormy eyes from his, she sat up. She poured oil into her palm and smoothed it on her arms and legs, becoming nervous as he stared at her, his eyes smoldering with tamped desire. She capped the bottle and sat silently, hands clasped around her knees, looking toward the sea—looking but not seeing—her thoughts centered totally on the magnetic pull of the man beside her—the first man to touch her heart or her body.

Nick lay propped on one elbow, his legs outstretched, their taut muscles and tanned skin a startling contrast to her pale satiny limbs. Eyes never leaving her face, he took his right hand and trailed a burning line with his fingers over the fine bone of her ankle, the swell of her calf, and the side of her rounded thigh. His fingers lingered on her hip until she squirmed to get away.

The palm of his hand across her stomach, he pushed her backward to the blanket. Her breasts heaved at his erotic touch; she lay tremulously, watching his eyes darken and his expression sober. Her lips parted, her dry throat constricted as he rolled his upper torso over hers. The hair on his chest felt sensually abrasive against her full breasts, the stimulus unbearably erotic.

His head descended, stopping above her lips for a long breathless moment, torturing her as she waited. With a throaty moan he took her mouth in a ruthless assault on her parted lips. His tongue probed relentlessly, demanding her participation, shuddering when he received it.

Her nerves screamed at his hungry embrace, but nevertheless she instinctively arched her hips, seeking closer contact. Her fingers clung to his shoulders and felt the warmth of his heated skin. Nostrils flared, she inhaled his clean, masculine scent. Her lips tasted the faint trace of salt left on his mouth from his swim. Delirious with desire, she gloried in the feel of his hands stroking her bare flesh, his firm mouth molding her throbbing lips.

Abruptly Nick raised himself.

Strong features outlined against the sky, he stared at the ocean, avoiding her questioning eyes. His biceps were taut and defined, as he sat with his arms clasped around his upraised knees. A faint sweat covered the muscles in his back as he spoke. "I'll never learn, will I, little one? It serves me right that I ache from head to toe. To put it bluntly, I throb with the pain of self-denial when I want desperately to feel you beneath me and make never-ending love to you."

Carlyn could see the primitive look in his eyes and feel the tension of emotion barely held in control that flowed between them like a hot current. She could feel a need for her own fulfillment also.

"I'm getting to where I can't even think straight when we're together," he exclaimed vehemently. "I'm consumed with the desire to possess, touch, taste. Your sweet scent seems to have permeated my brain." He turned to her, his eyes blazing with passion yet tender as he noticed the insecurity in her widened eyes. "Don't ever worry, darling. I will never knowingly hurt you in any way."

With a soft hand she reached impulsively to touch him. Her fingers stroked the side of his face in a loving caress, her eyes dark violet, expression ardent. Tracing his finely chiseled jaw, she slid both her hands over his neck and ran her fingers in his shiny hair. Raising, she arched toward him, her momentary fears forgotten as she yearned hungrily for another throbbing kiss.

Nick knew that if he gave in to Carlyn's lips he would not be able to deny his passion again. To squelch the tension of the moment he smiled childlike and said, "What kind of dog has no tail?"

Seeing the mischievous twinkle in his eyes, she retorted quickly, "A hot dog!"

"How did you know?" he teased, his expression crestfallen.

"Because I have a five-year-old nephew, which doesn't say much for your mentality and intelligent wit."

Nick's silly joke broke the deep emotion and they laughed together, temporarily banking their stirring passion.

Laying back, arms crossed beneath his head, Nick stretched his legs and closed his eyes to the heat of the sun. Striking up the conversation Carlyn had wanted to avoid, he asked her to tell him where she worked, what she did, and how she happened to be staying alone in the beach house.

Carlyn evaded telling an outright lie by saying she worked nearby, wherever her employer thought she was needed most, the location subject to change at any time.

Undeterred by her evasiveness, Nick persisted with his questions. "How do you happen to be staying here? I know the house is owned by an executive of a computer technology company. Are you a relative?"

"No."

"You must know him well, then."

"No. We have a casual aquaintance only," she answered honestly.

"How casual?" he persevered. "He has a wife and children."

"Yes, I know he is married, although I have never met his family."

"Why would any wife allow a beautiful young woman, whom she has never met, to stay in her home? Does she even know you're here?" he asked, raising his thick black lashes.

Lowering her eyes from his piercing gaze, she answered softly, "His wife doesn't know I'm staying here."

"What do your parents think of this?"

"My father doesn't know I'm here either. He lives in Oregon. My mother died when I was twelve. Any further questions, Nick?"

"Yes. A lifetime's worth at least. Are you an only child?"

"No. I have a very handsome brother," she replied, watching a distant surfer wipe out, his head plunging into a breaking wave. It was a momentary diversion from Nick's interrogation.

"Related to you he would have to be good-looking," Nick stated sincerely, staring at the beauty of her profile and the mane of shimmering hair. "How does your father earn his living?"

"He's retired, spends time fishing and enjoying his freedom from family responsibilities. He is a very energetic man and dedicated to his hobby of repairing radios. He has many that are very valuable, yet he refuses to sell a single one."

She hugged her knees, sitting comfortably on the blanket cushioned by the soft sand. A brief glance at Nick showed him listening intently to her family history. She continued telling the amusing incidents from her childhood, easily avoiding any incidents relating to her work as a police officer.

The bright sun caused her hair to glint with a blinding sheen as it tumbled about her bare shoulders, which were already taking on a faint golden tint. Her soft voice enchanted Nick as he lay beside her, anxious to know everything about her life prior to their meeting. Just looking at her alluring figure and captivating face made his loins ache as she told him proudly about her brother's mathematical genius and his doctorate in computer science.

In hopes of finding out more about her work, Nick questioned persistently. "Does you brother approve of your job?"

Carlyn glanced at him, startled at his query, but answered truthfully. "No, but then he knows little about what I actually do. He doesn't think my work is safe and he believes I am highly overpaid, though he is not aware of any specific details of how I earn my money." Carlyn felt her pulse quicken and eager to change the subject, she asked Nick to tell her more about his life.

Her twist did not go undetected—he was aware of her deliberate evasiveness. He rolled to his side and touched her stomach with his widely spread fingers. His hand was intimate on her soft flesh as he moved it over to the narrow width of her slender waist. Feeling the heat of her skin, he thought Carlyn had been sunbathing long enough, and he stood up. "Time to go in now, *cara*," he urged, his blazing eyes running possessively over the full length of her body.

She rose gracefully from the blanket, her hand holding his for support. Entranced by his voice and the closeness to his chest, she felt her heart pound. She swayed toward him, unable—and unwilling—to stay away, as she slowly moistened her dry lips with the tip of her tongue.

He watched beneath his lowered lashes, her provocative tongue drawing his eye. "Damn it, Carlyn. I'm trying to keep my hands off you and you seduce me with your innocent brand of magic."

With eyes lowered so that he wouldn't see her sudden need of him, her hand raised to his chest and her fingers twined the curly hair.

In a deep voice, he scolded adamantly, "My God, Carlyn, don't touch me so seductively. You're driving me wild." His hands reached for her as his head lowered, his breath wafting over her lips with a moan. "Kiss me, sweetheart."

Her lips parted to receive his kiss; her senses were inflamed immediately by the touch of his almost-naked body covered only by the brief swimsuit. Clasping his neck, she clung tightly, her breasts swelling against the warmth of his broad chest. She was shaken by his intense embrace, drugged by the masculine scent of his heated skin. Eager for his kiss, she made no objection when his hands slid down her naked back to her buttocks and drew her to his aroused body. She felt his legs spread so he could hold her to him more intimately.

Nick's lips stopped their relentless searching, and his mouth raised reluctantly. His body shuddering with desire, he held her to him, inhaling the aroma of her freshly washed hair as his hands slid up and down her spine, massaging her soft skin while she squirmed with delight. He trailed his tongue along her neck to her ear, lingering as he probed, his warm breath fanning her face. Suddenly he felt a sharp tug on his thick ebony hair. He nipped her earlobe sharply in retaliation, then laughed as she jerked away.

"Darn it, Nick, that hurt!"

"It was supposed to, wench. You've tugged my hair twice today and that hurt too," he explained, gathering the blanket and towel from the sand. "Besides, if you play with fire, you stand a chance of getting burned. You were definitely playing with fire when you tried to seduce me with the tip of your pink tongue moistening your soft lips. Be glad all you got was a little nibble on your earlobe." He grabbed her hand, then pulled her over the soft sand, amused by the mutinous expression on her face.

His infectious laughter and confident manner entertained her so, she giggled mischievously, "Are you taking me to dinner tonight?"

"My God, what happened to the good old days when women waited to be asked out?"

"They're gone forever. Think of all the good things women missed out on by being shy and retiring."

"Okay, I give up. I'll take you out and feed you tonight. Does a Big Mac and fries sound okay?" he quipped with humor.

"If I get a milk shake with it!" she retorted playfully.

"Be ready at seven. I've some business calls to make. Probably have to take out a loan too, as much as you eat." Ducking to avoid the handful of sand thrown at his broad back, he ran across the sand to his house, still laughing heartily.

She watched with shiny eyes the pronounced muscles in his deeply bronzed shoulders, his narrow masculine hips and straight, sturdy legs, until he was out of sight. She couldn't remember a time when she was more excited anticipating an evening. "Handsome beast knows how I feel too," she grumbled.

She ascended the stairs to the deck and walked straight to the bathroom. Eager to enjoy a leisurely bath, she shed her swimsuit, lay a long violet print silk lounging robe on the bed, and pinned her hair high off her neck before stepping into the tub. Relaxing, she let the water wash off the suntan oil and sand, but it could not wash away her tender thoughts of Nick. She lay back contentedly, soaking in the fragrant water.

The soothing sound of romantic music from the bedroom stereo lulled her into a sense of languor as the scented water caressed her naked curves.

CHAPTER FIVE

Nick's firm knocks unanswered, he entered the unlocked patio door. Calling Carlyn's name, he glanced in the living room and kitchen before ascending the stairs to the top floor. In the master bedroom he noticed a colorful robe draped on the king-size bed.

Curious as to her whereabouts, Nick peeked through the door of the bathroom. Her reflection in the mirror that surrounded the marble tub caught his eye immediately: she lay dozing luxuriously in the redolent foam of the bubble bath. He felt awed by her beauty and stared without shame at her partially exposed form.

Wavy hair curled in damp ringlets about her lovely face and glinted like polished silver in the light. Her lashes formed dark crescents on her cheeks above soft lips curved in a tiny half smile. Entirely visible in the slowly disappearing bubbles, her flawless breasts were full and pale, the pink nipples making him hunger to caress them with his mouth.

"Wake up, honey!" Nick coaxed huskily, taking a bath-sheet from the towel rack. "You'll catch cold if you stay in the water."

Startled by his unexpected appearance, she quickly drew both hands over her breasts and sank deeper into the water, blushing hotly. She glared fiercely, appalled by his audacity, her eyes flashing angry sparks at him. "Darn you, Nick! Get out of here this instant. I'm naked!" she cried excitedly.

"Now, that I had noticed myself and beautifully so," he added, infuriating her further as he made no move to leave nor to remove his interested glance from her naked body. Uncertain of what he was able to see through the few remaining bubbles, she grabbed the wet sponge from under the water and threw it at his smiling face.

But his reflexes were quick and he ducked the sponge, which splashed against the wall behind him. "Temperamental little mermaid, aren't you?" he drawled insolently, his eyes sparkling with amusement. "All that anger just because there's a man in your bathroom. If I had stripped and joined you, then you would have had cause for chagrin. Surely a glimpse or two of your creamy skin doesn't rate a wet sponge in the face. Lucky for you that you missed or I might have had to spank that pink little bottom, a chore I would have enjoyed immensely." Taking a step forward, he scolded, "Get out of the tub this minute or I'll let the water out and enjoy seeing the rest of your exquisite body."

As Nick reached to let the water out, Carlyn grabbed the bathsheet from his hand, pulling it into the tub to cover herself.

"Now look, you got your towel all wet and splashed water on the floor. I'll go to the living room for ten minutes, but if you aren't down by then, I'll return and dry you myself!" He turned to leave but glanced over his shoulder. "Another thing, keep your outside doors locked. No telling who might drop in uninvited," he teased laughingly.

"Oh! You . . . you . . . infuriating, horrible monster. I

hate you! Get out and make sure you stay out. I don't ever want to see you again. Why, you aren't even embarrassed by what you've done!" she spouted angrily, clutching the wet towel to her breasts.

"Not one whit, I agree . . . but then, I wasn't the one naked!" he mocked wryly. "The days of shock at the sight of a naked female are long past and at thirty-five I find it holds no mysteries. Of course, I must admit what I've seen of you thus far has been unequaled. *Arriverderci, mia cara,*" he whispered, nonchalantly leaving.

Her mind reeled from the blatant look of desire in his eyes and the seductive sound of his voice. Reining in her thoughts, she drained the tub and wrapped a dry towel sarong-fashion around her body. She peered cautiously into the bedroom, then rushed to the door, breathing a sigh of relief after she locked it.

Confident that Nick could not enter, she took her time drying her damp skin. Swift pats with a powder puff, an all-over spray of perfume, and she was ready to slip into her beige lace bra and matching bikini panties. Deciding the robe was adequate cover until she knew where they were going, she applied some makeup and brushed her hair until it fell in deep waves around her shoulders, noticing in the mirror the heightened color in her face from Nick's unexpected appearance.

The wet towel was thrown in the hamper and the stereo turned off before she unlocked the door and cautiously descended the stairs to the living room. Seeing no sign of Nick, she began to worry, remembering she had told him to get out, that she didn't want to see him again.

"Nick, where are you?" she called softly. When she did not receive an answer, her voice raised, the tone plaintive. "Nick! Quit fooling around. Oh . . . Nick, where are you?" Blinking back tears at the thought that he had left, she opened the door and stepped onto the wide deck.

Depressed, she walked to the deck railing hoping to see

him on the beach. The fog had rolled in, its gray dampness matching her mood, as tears trickled freely down her face. She was mad at her naiveté, because she knew that if she hadn't acted so angry he would have undoubtedly left immediately after determining that she was safe. In a childish gesture she wiped the tears from her cheeks with the back of her hand.

"Tears of joy or sadness, honey?" a voice behind her asked curiously. Startled, she quickly turned around. Nick casually appeared out of the dark, gloomy corner, holding a handkerchief in his outstretched hand. Placing his palms on her shaking shoulders, he scrutinized her expression carefully. "Don't tell me the thought of not seeing this infuriating, horrible monster again has upset you? I figured it would do you good to worry a little, but I didn't expect tears because of my absence."

Tilting her chin defiantly, she retorted coolly, "These aren't tears of sadness because you might not return but tears of regret that I might not get my Big Mac and fries!"

"Why, you mercenary wench, we'll eat at my house for that." He chuckled and hugged her briefly, enjoying the heady scent of her soft glowing skin. Gesturing at the dense fog settling around them, he ushered her into the living room and closed the door to shut out the cold.

"I have a better idea," she told him, her heart quickening at the sight of his well-groomed good looks. His broad chest was covered by a salmon-colored Lâcoste shirt, its snug fit hugging his sides. The partially unbuttoned neckline exposed the dark hair covering his chest. Thin white slacks clung to the muscles of his thighs, outlined his taut masculine hips as he turned and walked toward the fireplace.

"We can eat here tonight. I have the ingredients for something you've probably never tasted before."

"I very much doubt that. I've eaten at the finest restaurants in the world."

"Makes no difference. They won't have served this like I make it." As she started toward the kitchen she was stopped by Nick's voice.

"Come here, sweetheart. I haven't told you yet how gorgeous you look in that silk robe. It's very exciting the way it clings here and there as you walk. Come kiss me, Carlyn," he commanded softly.

Glancing backward over her shoulder, she realized that Nick was serious, that he expected her to return at his request. She glared, blurting out rebelliously, "I will not be ordered around by any man." Turning to face him, she stared defiantly.

"Little hellcat! You may scratch and fight now but I'll bet you'll be purring and obedient as a little kitten before I go home."

"Maybe, but you'll undoubtedly have a few claw marks too!" she sassed, her eyes wary as he walked up to her.

His piercing eyes holding hers, he demanded huskily, "Now kiss me!" She looked beautiful in her attempt to defy him, and he stared as if in a trance.

"I most certainly will not!" she retorted haughtily. "If you think you only have to command and I will obey, you're in for a surprise, Mr. Nicholas Sandini!"

Undaunted by her insurgence, he studied her rebellious face. "I said kiss me, Miss Carlyn Thomas!" His lean hands clasped her shoulders, his thumbs beginning a sensuous exploration over the thin material. Aware of her quivering reaction, he watched her eyes widen, bridled passion visible in their velvety depths. His hands moved from her shoulders to the nape of her neck, stroking her tender skin slowly. He took his time, deliberately watching her reaction, his hands relentless in their practiced seduction. Cupping her face in his broad palms, his head descended, but a breath away from her mouth he paused, his thumbs fondling the sides of her mouth, probing intimately. "Kiss me, sweetheart."

71

With his breath fanning her face, she lost all thought of feminine independence. She touched his mouth, initiating the caress, her parted lips placing featherlight kisses on his face. Her hands clung to his neck and she followed her instincts and rubbed his nape with soft fingers, stroked his unruly hair and the lobes of his ears.

Aroused the instant he felt her touch, he pulled her against the length of his body, becoming the leader. She became pliant and eager, her body molded to his taut contours. His mouth took hers in a deep, lingering kiss until she moaned with pleasure.

"Well, now that's much better. I think I've already managed to get a purr from my fiery hellcat," he teased tenderly before releasing her from his hold.

"No wonder you're not married. You're a chauvinist," she taunted, as she bowed down before him in a subservient manner. Giggling, she fled from the room, calling over her shoulder, "You really are a monster, and no free-thinking female would have you. That wasn't purring but my hungry stomach growling!"

Nick laughed at her impertinence but suddenly felt a chill in the room from the fog that clung damply to the glass wall. Taking kindling and papers from the filled woodbox, he knelt before the fireplace. He stacked them deftly, watching as they flared to life at the touch of a match. He added some dry eucalyptus logs, knowing that they would fill the room with warmth and that their pungent odor would pervade the air with a pleasant smell.

He kicked off his shoes and stretched out on the wide couch. His broad shoulders leaned against the end of the sofa as he watched the flames flicker, their iridescent colors changing from saffron yellow to fiery vermilion as the logs blazed hotly.

Carlyn's nostrils flared faintly as she entered the living room and inhaled the woodsy smell of burning logs. "Oh, how lovely. A fire always looks so peaceful," she whispered in a quiet, dreamy voice, glancing from the fireplace to Nick, stretched indolently on the couch.

She looked with pleasure at his finely shaped head resting on the arm of the couch. His ebony hair shone with vibrant health and cleanliness as it fell in waves over his forehead. Long sideburns added to the impact of his masculinity, dark against his high tanned cheekbones. Without raising himself, he let his eyes wander over her figure intimately, gesturing with his hand for her to join him on the soft cushions.

She seated herself gracefully. She reached for his left wrist and held it close to her face, checking the time in the dim glow from the burning logs. As she ran her fingers up and down his muscular arm, she teased, "Twenty minutes till our dinner is ready. Of course you're so lazy and hopelessly spoiled, you'll probably be asleep by then."

Nick sat up quickly and Carlyn feared she had offended him, but she soon discovered that he only wanted to sit with her cuddled close to his side. Stretching his long legs before him, he placed his stocking-clad feet on top of the heavy wooden coffee table. Carlyn positioned her shapely legs beside his, their thighs touching intimately as they sat close together.

The size of her small feet compared to his made her laugh and she remarked jokingly, "You have huge feet like my father and brother."

Pretending to be affronted, Nick pinched her shoulder and replied gruffly, "I would look silly walking around on your little feet. It takes a lot of foot to move six feet four inches of me around."

With a smile tugging her lips at his smug words Carlyn took her bare toe and slowly ran it up and down his ankle. The pink polish on her toenails stood out vividly against his white stocking.

Nick's hold tightened at her seductive touch. He drew her body to him until she was lying across his chest with her legs stretched along the cushions of the couch. "Passionate brat!"

He could feel her body tremble vibrantly against his broad chest. He let his eyes move possessively over her face, lingering on the rapid beat of the pulse at the base of her throat. Her silvery hair glimmered in the flickering firelight and splayed over his bronze arm in casual disarray. He raised a strand to his lips to inhale its sweet fragrance. "Umm, I like that," he whispered into her ear.

"I like it too," she agreed, twisting his words. "Wherever you touch me feels so good."

Carlyn was amazed by her frankness, but she so much enjoyed the new sensations she felt at Nick's touch that she let her instincts be her guide. She stroked his throat gently before sliding her hand in the open neck of his shirt. Letting her fingers spread through the thick mat of hair, she explored the broad muscles. Her nostrils filled with the scent of his freshly showered body and the pungent aftershave that had become so familiar to her.

"If you want to eat dinner, you'd better stop touching me, sweetheart," he warned, grabbing her exploring fingers and holding them immobile against his chest. He pinned her gaze with his darkened eyes. "Right now, I don't care if I ever see food again."

Tugging a handful of chest hair sharply, she mischievously retorted, "That won't last long with your appetite."

He scolded her for her impertinence by giving her a playful slap on the hip. "I was going to kiss you, but not now. You'll have to wait until after dinner." Running his glance over her impudent face, he taunted, "It's a good thing you're still young enough to train or you'd end up totally unmanageable. It appears that I'll have to take you in hand myself—just to keep some other poor devil from having the burdensome chore."

Carlyn quickly jumped to her feet, grabbed a couch pillow, and threw it at him as she raced toward the kitchen. Nick followed in hot pursuit. Breathlessly laughing, she told him to fill some tall glasses with iced tea while she assembled their dinner.

Obediently he prepared their drinks, mixing amber liquid with crushed ice and adding lemon wedges. He set the pitcher and glasses on the table, then seated himself as he watched her serve their dinner.

"What are these and how the hell do you eat them?" he asked, looking at the heaping plate set before him.

"Tostados and very carefully," she teased.

He took a cautious bite of the heaped tortilla but laughed as most of it fell back on his plate. "Hmm . . . let me see. Crisp-fried tortilla, lettuce . . ." he mimicked her comments on his marinated artichoke recipe.

"Refried beans spread on a crisp tortilla, then a heaping serving of seasoned ground beef, shredded lettuce, diced tomato, chopped onion, if you like, lots of shredded cheddar cheese, a heaping mound of guacamole and sliced black olives," she enumerated. "Oh, I almost forgot to serve my homemade hot sauce." She went to the refrigerator, then placed the dish on the table.

"I don't think there's room for another thing, but I'll see whether it's hot enough for my taste buds." He put a generous portion of the *salsa* over his tostado, then took another bite. "Absolutely perfect," he told her, coughing exaggeratedly, and reaching frantically for a gulp of iced tea.

They talked comfortably and ate the Mexican tostados, Nick pleasing her by asking for another. For dessert, Carlyn served the brownies. Nick cut a large square and chewed it with obvious enjoyment, while she finished her tea.

"Carlyn," he said, sitting back, "dinner was delicious. The tostados were unusual, actually quite tasty. I can see why you said your friends enjoyed them. They are different, delicious, and—looking down at the stain on his shirt

—amusing to eat. The guacamole was excellent. In fact, you have a blob of avocado dip on your nose." Nick wiped it off. "You go relax and I'll clean up the kitchen."

"That's fine with me," she agreed, watching as he placed their dirty plates in the dishwasher and cleared the table. Smiling smugly, she walked into the front room to wait on the sofa for him.

Nick entered the living room and walked directly to the fireplace. Squatting on his heels, he added a large log to the fire, then watched as the sparks flew upward. "Lazy wench. You were supposed to offer to help at least," he scolded humorously.

"I know, but the opportunity to get back at you for your masculine arrogance was too good to resist."

Nick went to the stereo, picked out a tape, and inserted it. Soft music filled the room with its romantic sound, adding to Carlyn's consciousness of their disturbing privacy.

He pulled her supple body effortlessly into his arms. Molded to each other, they danced slowly to the rhythmic sounds. His breath stirred the silky strands of hair beneath his chin as he bent to whisper against her ear. "Do you know how to do the elevator dance, honey?"

Lashes fluttering open, Carlyn raised her face, eyes soft and dreamy, thoughts languorous. "Umm . . . no . . . how's it done?"

"No steps," he replied seriously.

As it dawned on her she pushed against his shoulders. "That's so corny," she scolded. "I thought you were serious. For an adult you certainly have a weird sense of humor."

Undaunted, Nick stopped, enjoying Carlyn's volatile personality. Both hands clasped in the small of her back, he drew her hips against his body. "Put your arms around my neck, Carlyn," he demanded, his voice becoming husky with passion. As she complied he arched her body closer, feeling the touch of soft feminine lips caress the side of his jaw. Both hands fondled her lower back sensuously as he turned his face to look into the depths of her violet eyes for one long, poignant, heart-stopping moment.

"Now, isn't the elevator dance nice? You don't have to waste all that energy moving around." He lowered his mouth, their breath mingled as he murmured against her lips, "You feel so good pressed against the length of my body, your breasts so feminine and full, our thighs touching, your scent invading my nostrils. Does it feel good to you too, little one?"

"Umm . . . yes. I think this could become my favorite dance."

The feel of his aroused body tightly held in contact with hers, and his caressing fingers made her tremble with yearning for the feel of his skillful mouth. Outlining his lips sensually, teasingly, with her tongue, she was surprised when he pushed her away.

"Don't start that again. I made up my mind before dinner that kissing you was much too dangerous this early in the evening. In fact, dancing is much too dangerous this early in the evening."

"Too bad we don't have a chess set. That should keep you busy until after midnight!" she retorted, dismayed that he had stopped her.

"Excellent idea. I'll be right back." Before she could question him, he had left the living room and slammed out the front door.

Sitting on the fur rug before the fireplace, Carlyn clasped her upraised knees and waited for Nick to return. Within seconds he was back, had kicked off his shoes, and was sitting on the rug with the large coffee table between them.

She watched with amazement as he dumped a set of dominoes on the cleared surface and calmly mixed them up with both hands. "I hope you don't mind losing, as I intend to win each set," she teased mischievously, having played many times with her father.

"Ah, but I don't intend to lose, my sweet," he spoke confidently.

For the next two hours they played game after game, their laughter ringing through the room as first one would lose then the other. Finally, throwing up her hands in defeat, Carlyn pleaded for mercy. "I give up. You're the winner. But I still think you cheated. No one has ever beaten me three games in a row before."

Nick leaned back against the couch and looked at her, his mood suddenly serious. "What do I get for winning?"

"What do you want?" she taunted saucily.

"You!"

"Sounds fair," she returned boldly. "But since it was only by three games that you won, this will have to suffice." She stood up and walked around the coffee table, intending to place a brief kiss on his cheek.

"Oh, no, you don't, sweetheart," he whispered huskily as he pulled her down into his arms unexpectedly. "That little peck wouldn't satisfy the loser." Holding her across his lap, he moaned with frustration. "This is what I had in mind, *mia cara.*" He kissed her hungrily on the throat, ears, forehead, cheeks, and finally her soft vulnerable lips. His strong hands stroked her back, sending tremors of desire through her body.

Arching her back, she clung to his neck and pulled his mouth even closer to her lips, answering his probing tongue with a tentative flickering of her own, until she felt she was drowning in sensation. Moans of ecstasy came from deep in her throat when his hand teased the nipples of her breasts into hard buds of desire.

His searing kisses caused her blood to pound until she was aware of nothing but his devastating sexual drive. Unaware, she found herself gently lowered to the soft alpaca rug, shadows of the flickering yellow flames creating strange images.

Side by side, arms entwined, his mouth moving with possessive expertise, his experience bringing her to a state of rapture, he felt her surrender completely to his demands.

He rolled her onto her back, his hands exploring her body with gentle fingers. Her robe easily slid up as he stroked the long length of her silky thigh.

She lay unprotesting as he moved his fingers from her legs and unbuttoned the front of her robe. Pushing it aside, he trailed light kisses from her quivering lips to her arched throat, before searing the tender skin that formed the deep cleavage between her breasts. His warm breath and teasing nibbles drove her wild.

Separating the lace cups of her bra, he plundered the softness with his mouth. Her body shone in the glow of the burning logs as he cupped her breasts in his broad palms. His lips and tongue moved tenderly before he took possession of an erect nipple with his warm, hungry mouth in a caress that reached every nerve ending in her body.

She moaned softly, her vulnerable emotions responding violently to the magic of his hands and the moist warmth of his mouth. Her body aflame, she began to move under him sensuously.

Breathless at her response, Nick raised his mouth from her tender breast. Passionately he kissed her soft, sweet lips, already swollen from his lovemaking, as his hands cupped her face and his fingers threaded through her curls lovingly. Suddenly he sat up, his breath coming in short gasps, his body aching with hunger and unfulfilled desire.

Carlyn reached for him, unashamedly seeking his return, forgetting in her first moment of intense passion the morals of a lifetime.

He joined the cups of her bra over her breasts and rebuttoned her robe tenderly. "No, honey, I can't. If you weren't a virgin, I would have made love to you uncountable times already."

Looking at Nick, devouring him with her poignant gaze, she smiled understandingly. She noticed his eyes darken with desire as he whispered passionately, "I don't know when, honey, but next week, next month, or six months from now I will make you mine." He tenderly brushed the hair from her forehead. "I feel as if your very essence has invaded my soul, and to separate from you now would be to lose the other half of my heart."

Delighting in the feel of her hair, he continued to stroke the silky waves while he cradled her in his arms. As they embraced she reached for his hand and with physical yearning kissed the palm.

"No, honey, don't kiss me. I'm still a long way from being in complete control." Reluctantly raising his body from her side, he pulled her with him.

He towered over her as she stood beside him, her feet bare and hair tumbled from his caresses. His body shuddered as he looked at her slumberous eyes. "I'll come over tomorrow as soon as the fog lifts. We'll take a picnic lunch and go on a long drive up the coast to a favorite spot of mine. All you need to bring is yourself and a couple of brownies. Spending most of the day in the car should be easier on both of us."

With a brief kiss to her forehead he smiled grimly. "I'm much too old and experienced to stand this constant emotional turmoil and self-denial for much longer, so be forewarned, my purring kitten."

She watched wistfully as he left, making certain the door locked safely behind him.

Carlyn checked to make sure the fire was banked before walking slowly up the stairs to the empty bedroom. As she undressed and hung her robe in the closet, her thoughts were of Nick. She slid between the satin sheets prepared to enjoy a long contented night's sleep. But she was unaware how turbulently her emotions had been disturbed and how her body had been awakened to its womanhood by Nick's passionate lovemaking, and she couldn't understand the reason for her wakefulness.

The hours passed slowly as she tossed and turned restlessly. The fog was already lifting with the promise of a clear, sunny day when she finally drifted wearily into a deep sleep among the tumbled covers of her bed.

CHAPTER SIX

The phone rang sharply at nine thirty. Carlyn groped for the receiver and answered in a low, sleepy voice. "Nick . . . ?"

"My, my, I thought you'd be waiting impatiently to leave and instead I wake you! What happened? Did you miss me so much you spent the night pining for my presence?"

Not caught off guard, she retorted, "I admit I had a hard time falling asleep but not because of your absence, Mr. Sandini!"

"Don't feel bad, honey. I had a hell of a time getting to sleep myself. Must be building up a tolerance to cold showers. Any helpful suggestions to ease my pain?"

His deep timbred voice thrilling her, she cradled the phone, sassing impudently, "A long walk off a short pier?"

"Saucy brat in the morning, aren't you? I've been awake since six, jogged four miles, shaved, showered, and shopped. You, Miss Thomas, have ten minutes to get ready or I'll leave without you."

"Oh, no, Nick, give me half an hour or I won't bring the brownies."

"Okay, but that's blackmail!" Giving her an exaggerated smacking kiss, he laughed and hung up.

Within twenty-five minutes she had straightened the bed, showered, applied makeup, and was standing before the mirror fastening the narrow belt of her chocolate-brown sundress. Its white trim and buttons set off her faint golden tan. The deep veed bodice and narrow straps would be cool during the heat of the day, the matching jacket adequate protection for the evening.

Carlyn pushed her feet into strappy white sandals before racing down the stairs, a large straw purse swinging from her arm. Inhaling their rich chocolate aroma, she carefully packed four squares of chewy brownies in a plastic container with a tight-fitting lid. As she licked the frosting that clung to the spatula, she heard a knock at the door. She glanced at the clock and commended herself on her speed. *Leave it to Nick not to give me one extra minute*, she thought, opening the door to his impatient pounding.

Gray eyes lit with appreciation at the sight of her fresh beauty. Touching her darkly shadowed eyes with a fingertip, he murmured, "Poor sweetheart"—his voice soft and seductive—"you didn't sleep, did you?" He bent to her mouth and touched her lips briefly. "Umm . . . you taste like chocolate and smell like flowers. A potent combination."

As she observed him through lowered lashes, Carlyn's breath quickened. Nick wore beige jeans low on his lean hips. His short-sleeve dark brown cotton shirt was partially unbuttoned to expose a deep tan. Her stomach lurched when she caught the scent of his woodsy after-shave, so potent with his rugged masculinity.

"We match perfectly today." Her eyes questioning, he explained, "We're both wearing brown, which reminds me of chocolate, so be forewarned I might want a nibble or two of you during the day."

She returned to the kitchen to pick up her things, opting

to carry the jacket because of the morning heat. After she locked the front door, he put an arm around her waist and guided her to his Porsche, taking the brownies in his other hand.

"Apparently all you wanted was the brownies, but too bad, you have to take us both or none!" She chuckled, ruining her attempt to act affronted.

"Yikes, I'm found out. You'd better get in then, because I certainly don't intend to leave without the brownies." His eyes were drawn to a long length of naked thigh as she sat in the low bucket seat. Seated behind the wheel, he placed the key in the ignition before turning to help her fasten the seat belt. "Have you traveled along the coast before?" he asked curiously.

She glanced at him, a smile touching her lips. "Several times, but always rushed. My father's idea of a trip is to find the shortest route to a destination, rush there, then relax. I've always dreamed of rambling along during the day and stopping whenever the mood struck at night."

As they eased toward the gates of the colony, the motor purring with latent power, Nick's deep voice ran over her nerves like a caress. "I'll take you rambling anytime you wish if you'll agree to share the nights with me. Okay, *mia cara?*"

"The days sound fine but I don't know if I'm ready for the nights yet," she teased as they exchanged smiles.

"Yes, you are, sweetheart," he assured her sensuously. "Ready, unwilling, and able!"

The guard looked envious as Nick and Carlyn drove past, waving in answer to their upraised hands. Turning north, the Porsche hugged the road closely as it sped along the winding highway.

Between houses Carlyn caught brief glimpses of the ocean. Luxurious estates on landscaped acreage alternated with clustered rentals on tiny plots of sand. She relaxed as the road veered inland several miles before returning to the shoreline.

Nick took his right hand from the steering wheel and placed his lean fingers on Carlyn's knee, squeezing it lovingly. His brief glance took in her rapt expression. "Having fun, darling?" he asked huskily.

His casual endearments and deep voice gave her pleasure and she turned to him, her violet eyes shining with happiness. "Yes, Nick, a wonderful time." The touch of his fingers on her bare skin caused her flesh to burn. Her lashes lowered to block the desire she knew would be visible in her expressive eyes.

As Nick slowed to pass through the lovely coastal city of Santa Barbara, Carlyn noticed numerous girls hitchhiking alone. Holding up cardboard signs crudely painted with their destinations, they were easy prey for some sociopath.

Aware of the thousands of runaways in Los Angeles who wanted freedom from their parents, but ended up slaves to drug peddlers, perverts, and pimps, she shuddered. It had been her heartbreaking task uncounted times to notify distraught parents and to counsel confused teenagers who had got into horrendous situations they couldn't handle.

"What's the matter, honey?" Nick inquired, having noticed her frown and shudder.

Carlyn shook her head. "Nothing, other than the depressing aspects of my job."

"The one you won't tell me about?" he probed seriously.

Ignoring his question, she watched as he turned inland to the east, rising rapidly into rugged brush-covered hills. The air immediately became drier as they left the beach for the interior valley region.

Nick geared down for a sharp turn prior to pulling into a view area above the small dam across Lake Cachuma.

He smoothly stopped the Porsche and turned to her. "Like my shortcut to our destination?" Pleased at her agreeing nod, he smiled.

Too excited to wait for him to open her door, she stepped out and walked to the edge of the path. A hot breeze whipped strands of hair around her face as she looked below her at the irregular border of the inland lake. The rugged hills to the east were barren and desolate despite the pungent smell of manzanita bushes and scrub oak thick on the western border. An indignant ground squirrel scolded her furiously for interrupting his search for food. Laughing at his antics, Carlyn was unaware when Nick approached.

He crossed his arms over the front of her body and lowered his head to nuzzle her gleaming hair, while she leaned back against his broad strength. Several minutes passed in total silence as they stood in contentment. He placed a kiss on her tumbled hair before guiding her back to the Porsche. "Come on, lazy bones. We've many miles to travel," he told her amicably but followed the kind words with a sharp swat on her buttocks when she protested.

Amused by his commanding attitude, she rushed to the car and was seated with her seat belt fastened by the time he had eased his long length behind the wheel.

"For a moment out there I thought I had a submissive, docile, traveling companion in my arms, but instead you have reverted back to your sassy, impertinent true self," he teased, chuckling at her humorous defiance.

They left the rugged mountains by descending into the rolling hills of Santa Ynez Valley. Acres of white rail fences, sprawling luxurious ranch houses, and ostentatious barns attested to the area's wealth.

Nick stopped beside a pasture to let Carlyn look. Expensive Arabians, Thoroughbreds, and quarter horses stood in the shade of large oak trees. Head to tail, necks outstretched resting, they switched flies, uncaring of their human observers. Young foals frolicked on long agile legs, slept in the hot sun, or greedily nursed their dams. All were a delight to watch.

"I'm having a lovely day, Nick. An absolute perfect time," she whispered dreamily as he pulled back onto the highway.

"Wonderful, sweetheart. That was my intent." Nick pointed left as they passed a turnoff. "We're only a couple of miles from the town of Solvang. It's a Danish village with fascinating decor and bakeries filled with mouth-watering pastries, but too interesting to be rushed."

Enthralled by their trip and Nick's compelling personality, Carlyn relaxed in the deep leather seat. She stared at Nick's lean, tanned hands, the fingers long, the nails spotless and clipped. His strong profile and sharply defined jaw seared her with longing. His eyes never left the road as she continued her scrutiny undisturbed. Unbidden thoughts of being held to his broad chest, the rapture of her lips being crushed beneath his hard mouth in searching, hungry kisses tortured her.

"Quit it, Carlyn," he reprimanded her, not even turning his head.

"Quit what?" She stiffened and turned to look out the window.

"Seducing me with your eyes and thoughts. I'd rather be kissing you too," he told her calmly, correctly reading her mind.

Flushed, she lowered her head, hands clasped tightly in her lap. "Where are we going, Nick?" she queried to change the subject.

"I'm cutting back to the coastal highway now enroute to our destination of Pismo Beach. Have you been there?" The corners of his mouth lifted, his brief glance tender.

Aware of the suppressed passion in his steely eyes, she

shook her head. "No, but I've heard of the giant Pismo clams."

Grapevines stood in even rows over the rolling hills. Grazing land with herds of fat beef cattle soon gave way to thousands of acres of flat irrigated fields. Dark green broccoli and white cauliflower cradled in silvery leaves grew abundantly in the rich loamy soil as they continued north on Highway One.

A profusion of eucalyptus trees each side of the narrow road filled the car with their pungent aroma, reminding her of their passionate lovemaking before the fire the previous night.

"Watch closely now, sweetheart," Nick told her, gearing down for a sharp curve. He slowed; his eyes flicked to hers, checking her reaction.

The view was one Carlyn knew she would always remember. The town of Pismo Beach was nestled in the distance along the edge of a broad, curved bay, whose beaches were long and flat. The deep vivid blue of the calm ocean was breathtakingly clear. Mammoth ever-changing sand dunes were visible to the south, looking like a setting for an Arabian Nights movie.

Nick's deep voice broke her silent contemplation as he wound down the steep road. "First time I rounded this corner the fields were covered with seed flowers in full bloom. The color and fragrance were overpowering. The last few years there has only been row crops. Not as pretty to see but much tastier."

In minutes Nick had turned toward the beach and to Carlyn's shock drove the Porsche over a wooden ramp and directly onto the firm sand. Turning away from town, he drove south until they were far from the cluster of houses and small businesses. He stopped the car with its sleek silver nose facing the sea, the broad tires resting on the damp sand.

Nick stretched his wide shoulders, relaxing after the

long drive, as they both inhaled the moist salty air. "This is it, honey." He turned, his hand clasping her knee. "We're in dune-buggy country now."

As he spoke, his thumb rubbed her knee, his fingers resting on the smooth skin of her inner thigh. Electricity from his intimate touch coursed through her body. Carlyn fought the desire for his affectionate touch to change to passion. She quivered with the thought of his fingers stroking the full length of her leg.

Aware of her emotions as she trembled, he removed his hand, running his glance possessively over her body, resting it on her full breasts, as he whispered, "Not yet, honey. We have all afternoon."

Embarrassed, she quickly asked, "Have you ever driven a dune buggy, Nick?"

"Many times. On Fourth of July and Labor Day weekends this area looks like the Los Angeles freeway. To keep the buggies from running into each other they have high antennas with tiny bright-colored flags mounted on the back. It's great sport."

"Can we get out and walk around?"

"You can walk all you like after we have our picnic. You didn't offer me breakfast and I'm starved!" Nick grabbed a blanket and bamboo picnic hamper from the back, telling Carlyn to bring the brownies.

As she tried to match his long strides, Nick led her over the soft dry sand until he found a spot against the rising dunes. Protected by wild grass on either side, it gave them complete privacy but still afforded a broad vista of the flat beach before them.

Nick removed his shoes and socks while Carlyn kicked off her sandals. Both enjoyed the feel of the warm sand beneath their bare feet as they bent to straighten the blanket.

Nick spread his arms wide as he explained to Carlyn about the giant Pismo clams. "During the proper season the beach is crowded with people digging clams. The local shops sell licenses, rent digging forks, and even supply you with a recipe for clam chowder."

A soft breeze stirred the hem of Carlyn's skirt about her shapely figure as she stood viewing the area with rapt expression. Nick felt a surge of desire course through his body as she stood outlined against the dunes. It was all he could do to resist the temptation to pull her into his arms and onto the soft sand and enjoy the taste of her yielding lips. "Let's sit down and eat," he commanded gruffly.

Carlyn complied, tucking her legs to the side as she watched Nick, aware of his darkened eyes and sensing his heightened emotions.

His voice arrogant, he teased, "Watch my every move so on our next picnic I can relax and you can wait on me." Unwrapping two fresh-baked French rolls covered with sesame seeds, he split them lengthwise and sprinkled on an oil and vinegar dressing. He piled on thin slices of salami, mortadella, ham, provolone cheese, and pepperoni before adding sliced tomatoes, lettuce leaves, and peppers. He wrapped the sandwich in a large napkin and handed it to Carlyn.

"I could never eat all that!" she blurted out as she took it from him.

"Eat what you like, the gulls can eat the rest," he told her, reaching in the basket for a bottle of red wine and one crystal glass. He filled it, smiling mischievously. "We have to share, which was my purpose for only bringing one glass."

She took a small sip, enjoying the robust taste, then handed the glass to Nick. She watched as he deliberately turned it so his mouth was placed where hers had been.

His eyes held hers as he drank slowly, sensuous awareness darkening his pupils. "My God, but I want to make love to you!"

Carlyn flushed, tearing her eyes from his as she contemplated Nick as a lover. She knew instinctively, through his many courtesies and constant consideration for her comfort, that he would be a tender lover and could bring her undreamed-of delights.

He looked at her, aware of her embarrassment. "I won't rush you, *mia cara*. When you're ready, you'll ask me, then we'll both reach heaven in each other's arms." Telling her to eat her sandwich, he leaned back on the blanket, legs stretched out before him. "Delicious, isn't it?" he asked, watching her take small bites but chewing hungrily.

"Very, as you expected it to be." She wrapped the uneaten portion in her napkin after wiping her hands and mouth. Sated, she lay on the blanket, her hands pillowing the back of her head. Her sundress clung to her full breasts and narrow waist as she closed her eyes in utter contentment.

She heard Nick open the plastic container. Her eyes raised in time to see him place a brownie to his lips with a look of anticipated pleasure in his keen eyes. "Pig! Give me a bite. I haven't even tasted them yet," she scolded playfully.

"Since you insist." He leaned toward her, dangling the rich sweet over her mouth. "Open wide and I'll feed you."

"You goof. More than likely you'd choke me." Holding his wrist with one hand, she broke off a piece with the other. She chewed it slowly, then stretched indolently to enjoy the sun's rays on her skin.

He watched her graceful movements, his ebony hair shining in the sun, then lay on his side next to her. Leaning over, he took his tongue and licked a crumb of brownie from the corner of her mouth. "Much better than a napkin," he insisted, his voice hoarse with need, impatient to touch her again.

Carlyn's heart suddenly missed a beat, aroused by the intimate touch with his tongue. She wiggled in a vain attempt to break contact with his hard male chest. She noticed every detail of his face poised above her: tiny laugh lines at the corners of his eyes, the unruly wave of hair over his forehead, the firm mouth that could raise her to such heights wherever it touched.

"Lie still! It's too late to get away now." He buried his face in her neck as his broad shoulders shook. "Oh, God, sweetheart, you look so soft and feminine. The scent and feel of you is driving me out of my mind." With gentle hands he ran his fingers through her tumbled hair before cupping her face in his palms. Nick's breath quickened with desire when his lips came in contact with Carlyn's mouth. With leisure he nibbled the corners of her trembling lips, his tongue flicking the edge of her teeth as he turned his face.

Unable to stand the torment of his seductive teasing, Carlyn began to murmur deep in her throat. Bare slender arms reached to pull his head down, to force his lips to stay on her seeking mouth. Her composure was in complete chaos; she encouraged his passion.

"Damn it, Carlyn, why are you so sensual, so responsive to my touch?" His words spoken, Nick raised a fraction away from her tight hold. "The purpose of this trip was to cool our relationship down. You're not helping one bit."

"Kiss me, Nick," she pleaded, ignoring his harsh censure.

The rapid beat of her pulse pounded beneath the pad of his thumb as he touched her throat. "You asked for this, and by God, you'll get it!"

In a deep, throaty voice he moaned words of love before his mouth seized hers in a kiss that burned every nerve from head to toe. His mouth took its toll of her sensitive lips as his hands moved intimately on both breasts, across the trembling softness of her stomach, and came to rest clasping her upper thigh.

Carlyn arched her body toward Nick's hips, wild with

the urgent need to caress him. Her nostrils flared daintily as she breathed deep of his heated skin. With eager fingers she unbuttoned his shirt and lightly ran them across his broad chest. The rapid beat of his heart inflamed her—she gloried in her effect on him. Whispering his name over and over, she felt his mouth leave her lips to plunder her neck before trailing downward to her burgeoning breasts.

Nick placed his knee between her legs as his lean fingers slid the length of her body. Palms trembling at the feel of her bare thigh, he pushed her skirt aside in his quest to touch every inch of satiny leg. When his fingers touched the lace edge of her panties, he slid them under the material, his hand intimately cupping the firm smoothness of her rounded buttocks. Her slender body was supple as he drew her hips against his rock-hard flesh, feeling his every fiber quiver with longing. Her murmurs of pleasure were silenced by the continuous plundering of her mouth in fierce, turbulent kisses.

His hand released her buttocks to stroke over her body to her breasts, easily slipping off the narrow strap of her bodice. Her full, mature breast cupped in his palm, he lowered his face, nuzzling her low-cut bra aside to take the rosy nipple into his mouth. Her body shuddered, the enticed peak hardening and swelling to the flicking of his tongue and warmth of his mouth.

Her deep moans of intense physical pleasure while his mouth worshiped her breasts brought him to his senses. With reluctance he drew away, only to bury his face against her neck, until his own control was tamped temporarily. His shaking fingers pulled her dress over her swollen breasts.

As he kissed her mouth tenderly, lightly, his gentleness caused tears to trickle from her stormy, dilated eyes. Carlyn felt overcome by emotion for Nick.

He removed her clinging fingers, awed by the look of yearning and love in her exquisite face. Aching with the need to possess her, he found it nearly unbearable to rise to his feet. He took her hands and pulled her up, balancing her quivering body until she regained her composure from his tumultuous lovemaking.

"I think we'd better go on our walk now," Nick said, clearing his throat. "We should have brought the dominoes or at least picked a day when the beach wasn't so deserted."

He gathered their picnic debris and blanket, then took Carlyn's hand and walked to the car. As he bent to place the hamper on the backseat, his muffled voice challenged her to a race. He rolled up his pant legs in time to hear Carlyn's laughter as she fled along the firm sand. Bare feet splashing in the surf, Nick found himself stretched to the limit as he raced after her fleet figure.

As soon as she felt his firm hand grab her, Carlyn, giggling helplessly, stopped. They stared at each other, catching their breath after the long run, letting the wavelets trickle over their feet.

"Pretty fast for a female, aren't you, love?" he mocked. Then, to quell her arrogant pride for making him take so long to catch her, "Your fifty-foot head start helped though."

"I have to be in good physical shape for my job," she explained, forgetting her vow to evade his questioning.

"With your figure you should be the president of the mystery company," he retorted, leering mischievously at her shapely curves as she stood at arm's length.

"Not that kind of shape!" She glared at him. "*Condition* is a better word." Lowering her lashes, she spotted several large white clam shells. "Help me, Nick. I want to take some of these huge shells back to my little nephew, Billy." She bent to gather one and enjoyed the feel of the smooth white interior and rough pale outer shell. On the way back to the Porsche Carlyn found several unbroken shells, while Nick grumbled because he was delegated to carry them to the car.

"I knew it. A female has all the fun while the male does all the work." He grinned wryly. "My God, not driftwood too!" he exclaimed as she added pieces of bleached wood.

Thick lashes fluttering rapidly, she flirted in a bold manner. "You say you're a chauvinist, so quit groaning over a few light pieces of driftwood and sea treasures."

"Your flirting won't entice me this time. Good thing for me I didn't take you to northern California. Entire trees, some weighing tons, wash up on the beaches, and you'd probably want one of those for little Billy too."

As Nick put the shells and driftwood in a sack behind the seat, she remembered her uneaten portion of sandwich. Their laughter intermingled with the cries of the greedy gulls that boldly hovered near them to get the scraps. Their screeches were loud and fierce as they fought among themselves before flying away abruptly when their unexpected food supply ended.

Seated in the car, after slipping into their shoes, Nick put the key in the ignition. Carlyn's touch on his arm, her plea to sit and look at the view, stopped him. With his head leaning against the door, he enjoyed the sight of her lovely profile.

As she watched the foamy surf slip relentlessly over the wide flat beach, she asked wistfully, "Where do you live permanently, Nick?"

"Not Malibu. That house is owned by my ex-college roommate and best friend, Brett Masters. We exchange houses when it's convenient. He's a psychiatrist. In fact he owns several clinics, lectures, and writes technical books."

Carlyn watched Nick, listening intently to each word, wanting to know everything about his past life.

"I have three homes," he continued. "An apartment in New York City, convenient to stay in when I have business on the East Coast. My major residence is a home in the Twin Peaks area of San Francisco. It's built on four levels, each with a clear view of the bay and the Golden Gate Bridge. It's quite formal and is excellently cared for by a live-in couple who have been with me for years. I'm never in my New York or San Francisco homes for very long since I'm ordinarily traveling between restaurants, although my main office is in San Francisco."

Nick put his arm around her and kissed her forehead. Urged to continue by her rapt expression, he smiled, his tone changing as he spoke of his last home.

"My true home, the place I go if I have a problem to settle or feel the need for total isolation, is a couple hundred miles north of San Francisco. Several years back I purchased five hundred acres deep in the giant redwoods, high on a hill overlooking the rugged shoreline. It's my heaven on earth. I designed and built the house myself and furnished it with only *my* pleasure in mind. Two stories tall, with wide decks that jut into the spiny needles of the redwoods, it blends with its surroundings perfectly."

With an intense glance he surveyed the beauty of her tumbled silvery hair. "I'm quite a distance from the shoreline but high enough so that the view is fantastic. I picked the building sight so I wouldn't have to remove any trees —I'd commit mayhem on anyone who did. A pollution-free stream runs by the house into a three-acre fish-stocked pond. I intend to retire there, grow fat and bald, and watch the world go by from a lounge on my deck. I have refused to put a telephone in, nor have I a television set. If I want to know what's happening in the outside world, I have to drive down the mountainside to the nearest town, Fort Bragg, and buy a newspaper."

With his left hand he tilted her face up toward his so that their eyes met. His thumb stroked her lower lip as he said seriously, "It has a king-size bed that only I have slept in. Would you like to be the first woman to share my love nest in the hills?"

Shaken by his statement and probing thumb, she turned away, refusing to answer. Her head lay on his shoulder, drawn there by his hand.

Fingers stroking the silky threads of hair he eased the tension aroused by his intimate question by suggesting they watch the sunset before leaving.

Her hand lay on his strong thigh, the muscles tightening as her fingers trailed to his knee. But she felt unsatisfied: she wanted to explore all of his lean body, to touch each well-sculpted muscle. Suddenly fearing reproach, she jerked her trembling hand away, intent on moving back to her side of the car.

"No, Carlyn! Touch me wherever you want," he groaned, dragging her back into his arms. "Just one kiss, honey, before we leave." He took her hand and held it on his chest over the rapid beating of his heart.

She touched her mouth to his neck, her lips trailing across his throat. Both arms raised, clinging to his nape, her mouth sought his firm lips, eager for his tempestuous caress and the pulsating whirl of pleasure that followed.

Against her mouth he whispered passionately, "I want you so bad, darling. So damn bad!"

His mouth bruised her soft lips as he parted them, hungry to seek the nectar within. Tongue probing, he kissed her with such devastating desire, her mind reeled with pleasure, her senses clamored for fulfillment. Her vulnerability to his sexual expertise made her a willing conquest, as she responded fervently.

He tore his mouth from hers reluctantly, kissing her forehead before clasping her face to his heaving chest. The heat of his body matched her flushed cheeks as she heard him murmur before pushing her away, "We're too isolated here, honey, and I have a blanket in the back—both powerful temptations with you so responsive to me."

His hand raised to her face, smoothed the tumbled curls from her forehead with trembling fingers. "You'd better

97

fasten your seat belt by yourself, Carlyn. If I put my hands on your waist, I'll make love to you until the sun rises."

Nick switched on the motor and accelerated rapidly, causing the wheels to spin in his anxiety to remove them from the temptation of their isolated setting. Sand was flung in a wide arc as the powerful car raced over the firm beach, up the ramp, and onto the road south.

Miles passed rapidly, but Carlyn was quiet, her slender fingers clasped, her emotions still dazed from the passion so easily aroused. *His touch is like a drug,* she thought. *As potent and addictive as an upper.*

She looked up in surprise as Nick slowed down in the town of Guadalupe. Carlyn remembered passing through it on the way to Pismo Beach. It had appeared to be a sleepy rural village then but the sidewalks were now filled with local inhabitants. They sauntered or lounged, in front of the brightly lit bars, restaurants, or all-night poker parlor, relaxing after working the nearby fields.

Nick made an abrupt turn into a small parking area to the left of a two-story unadorned, plastered building with a bright neon sign announcing FAR WESTERN TAVERN.

"What's here, Nick?" Carlyn asked curiously.

"Our dinner," he answered quickly, pulling the low Porsche between a dust-covered Chevrolet pickup and a shiny new luxurious Lincoln Continental. "Actually I'm lucky tonight. I usually have to park on the street. Their food is so popular with local residents and well-known by tourists that the parking lot rarely has an empty spot during the dinner hour."

"I've never been here. What do they serve?" she asked, gathering her purse as Nick opened the passenger door.

"Good food and lots of it." He locked the car carefully, then, because of the brisk ocean breeze filled with a hint of the fog to come, helped her into the short jacket that matched her sundress.

Nick placed a possessive hand on Carlyn's elbow as they

walked through the entrance directly into the saloon. The darkened room was filled with people, either sitting at the forty-foot L-shaped oak bar, or along the wall fronted by tiny cocktail tables. The tinny sound coming from an old-fashioned nickelodeon added to the Western atmosphere.

Carlyn's eyes sparkled with pleasure as she looked at Nick. "I like it." She returned his smile, then scanned the people curiously. Men in business suits and handmade shoes rubbed elbows with cowboys and ranchers in denim jeans, faded shirts, and cowboy boots.

"This building was originally a hotel built in 1912, and the bar was supposedly shipped around the Horn at the beginning of this century. Let's go wash up, then have a drink," he suggested, dropping his brief explanation of the restaurant's history quickly.

Returning from the rest room, hair smoothly brushed around her shoulders, makeup freshened, Carlyn smiled as Nick pulled her to his side and asked what she wanted to drink. Seated on a tall barstool with his body protectively close behind her, she glanced at him over her shoulder. "Other than an occasional glass of wine, I don't drink, Nick." Aware of the many admiring glances directed at Nick's commanding size and striking good looks, she felt proud.

"You don't drink, don't smoke, and you're a virgin. Sounds too good to be true," he whispered huskily in her ear, his hand grasping her narrow waist possessively.

Carlyn raised her chin, retorting impudently, "How do you know I don't smoke? In fact, you don't know about my purity either," she whispered as she saw the bartender approach.

Nick ordered a gin and tonic, then turned her around to face him, his head bent to her ear. "First, I know you don't smoke because I can smell the clean aroma of your hair and skin. Second, despite your eager passionate response to my lovemaking, your eyes lack sexual knowledge." He sipped his drink slowly, indifferent to any woman but Carlyn. His eyes never left her face, amused by her embarrassment at his blatant interest. *God, she's lovely,* he thought with tenderness.

Paged from the dining room, Nick guided Carlyn by the waist. "I'm glad to get you out of there. Too many single men looking at you and thinking the same things I am. You're much too alluring for my peace of mind."

They passed through the cut-glass adorned doors that led into the main dining room, following their waitress to a table along the far wall. The room was bright and immaculately clean, yet simple and appealing. The windows were framed with swag drapes made from tanned Hereford cowhide. The rich red-brown and white hair was unique and fit perfectly with the Western pictures adorning the light-colored walls. Bright red cloths covered the tables. Place mats were paper, napkins sparkling white linen, silver plain and unadorned.

In the center of the table was a basket of assorted crackers, a crockery dish of butter squares, and a pressed-glass relish tray—filled with iced crisp celery, green onions, carrot sticks, radishes, peppers, pickles, and black olives—beside a dish of homemade *salsa.*

Carlyn studied the large menu, uncertain what to order, yet surprisingly hungry.

Noticing her quandary, Nick prompted, "The specialty is 'Bull's Eye' steak—incidentally, it's their own patented trademark—but they also serve lobster. What would you prefer, *cara?*"

"Both!"

"Me too," he agreed readily. "As you know, you give me a hell of an appetite—sometimes even for food!" He broke off the intimate conversation as the waitress approached to take their order.

Too hungry to wait for dinner, they nibbled on the fresh

relishes. Carlyn followed Nick's example and buttered a cracker, putting a spoon of *salsa* on it. She chewed it thoughtfully, then looked up smiling. "It's excellent," she told him, taking another spoonful.

"But not hot like the sauce you blistered my mouth with on the tostado," he teased, telling her to keep her place mat, as the recipe was on it, if she wanted to make some herself.

Indifferent to the other diners, they talked between each bite as Nick ate a hearty bowl of onion soup and Carlyn speared another bit of her bay shrimp cocktail. Next came crisp mixed-green salads. Thirsty after their long walk along the beach, they sipped their second glass of iced tea.

"Oh, Nick, not all this too!" Carlyn exclaimed when their waitress set the entrée before them. The "Bull's Eye" steak was thick and tender. A boneless rib-eye of beef, supplied by the nearby Corralitos Ranch and marinated in Far Western's own spices, it was grilled over California live oak and served sizzling hot. Succulent lobster and drawn butter was nestled next to a baked potato heaped with sour cream and chives. A side dish of brown chili beans made a spicy, delicious addition, as did the hot garlic bread wrapped in a napkin to keep it warm.

They conversed with an easy rapport, Carlyn entranced by Nick as she listened to each word. Her expressive eyes revealed the complete surrender of her untouched heart to his keeping.

As a tender smile crossed his face, his hand reached for Carlyn's, his mind reeling with the fact that he had found the one woman he would be willing to devote his life to. A woman he had never expected to meet after his years of brief, meaningless encounters.

"Did you enjoy our trip?" he asked, his fingers stroking the back of her hand with a loving gesture.

"I loved it," she answered softly, a dreamy look changing her violet eyes to deep velvety purple.

"Everything?"

"Everything," she answered truthfully. His voice had lowered, to a deep husky murmur, eyes darkening to charcoal-gray, reminding her of his sensuous caresses and her uninhibited response. She lowered her lashes to shield her burgeoning love. She knew the sudden longing to be back in his arms would be visible in their depths. "Everything, Nick."

"Good! That's the way it should be," he told her emphatically. "Ready for dessert now?" he inquired. He turned her hand over, rubbing her palm, aware she was disturbed by his caress.

"No . . . I couldn't eat another thing." Sliding her hand from under his, she told him. "I'm totally satisfied."

"I'm not."

"Stop it, Nick." She flushed, understanding his meaning instantly. "You act insatiable."

"I am—for you!" He motioned for their waitress, ordering two desserts. Vanilla ice cream for Carlyn, raspberry for himself.

Much too full to eat anything else, she gave her ice cream to Nick, her eyes sparkling with amusement at his boyish expression. "You pig. You ordered vanilla ice cream for me just so you could mix it with your sherbet!"

"Right on the first try," he admitted, enjoying the cool dessert with obvious delight. Finished, he left money for the bill plus a generous tip. "Let's go, honey, we've a long drive home."

"I don't think I could find my way back without a map, since you kept switching highways," she told him, walking to the car. Suddenly sad that their day was nearing an end, she fought with the desire to confess her love. She ached to tell him she wanted to share his life—the good times like today, as well as those less perfect. His masculine appeal and vigorous strength, with a keen mind and sense of humor, had wrought irreparable changes to her inner peace. She knew she would find it unbearable to live without his stimulating company. His deep voice interrupted her meditation with abrupt suddenness.

"Don't worry about it. I'll act as chauffeur wherever you want to go. Actually, most people drive here from Highway 101, through Santa Maria on California Route 166, but I prefer taking Highway One through Los Alamos. I enjoy the rural countryside in all its seasons."

Returning to the main highway, Nick accelerated the high-powered engine, the responsive Porsche seeming to cover the deserted road as if it had wings. Nick placed an eight-track tape in the stereo, and the sound of soft music filled the car.

Carlyn's long sleepless night took its toll. Within minutes the warmth of the car and the music had lulled her to sleep. Her head lay comfortably on Nick's broad shoulder.

Nick's nostrils filled with the perfume of her hair, his pulses stirred. Carlyn's hand rested on his thigh as her soft body leaned against him, adding to his need for physical release.

He reflected on his past life seriously. An active, virile man, he had not led a celibate life since his teens. He made certain his companions were aware of his views by explaining explicitly the rules he lived by. Despite their knowledge that they would never have a permanent relationship, he had his pick of many beautiful sophisticates. The women clamored for his attention, as he was generous with his money and an ardent, unforgettable lover. If their attitude became serious or demanding, he walked away without a backward glance, his emotions never touched.

With a tender expression Nick looked briefly at Carlyn, knowing he had found his woman, the one woman in the world he desired a permanent relationship with.

He admitted his hypocrisy, knowing he had made love to countless women through the years, yet expecting Carlyn to be a virgin. His blood pounded with jealousy at the thought of anyone just touching her. He knew he would want to kill any man who dared possess her innocent body, wanting to be first himself.

Nerves tightening at the thought of parting from her when they arrived in Malibu, he gripped the steering wheel until his knuckles were white. The knowledge that he could easily seduce her into lovingly giving him her innocence that night caused his broad shoulders to shudder.

Since he met Carlyn, Nick had continuously denied himself the satisfaction his body craved. Groaning, he thought of another long restless night without sleep. A night haunted by the memory of her exquisite face and sensuous responsive body. He decided to tell her the next morning of his love, certain she felt the same.

He stopped the Porsche in the hazy moonlight, touching her closed eyelids with a tender kiss.

Sleepy, she barely felt Nick's gentle caress before she raised her face to seek his mouth. An action as natural as if she had been awakening beside him for years.

His traitorous body surged with desire and her hands clung to his shoulders as he kissed her soft parted lips. Seeking the urgency of his mouth with matching hunger, she melted against him, instantly responsive to his touch.

He took her arms from his neck, scolding playfully, "Come on, sleepyhead. You're obviously half asleep or you wouldn't play with fire by climbing all over me. Besides, you probably crippled me for life by lying on my shoulder all the way home. It was a wonder I could drive."

Immediately contrite, Carlyn asked softly, "Did I really hurt you, Nick?" Her eyes sought reassurance as she tried to see his face in the darkened interior of the car.

He smiled but replied seriously, "Never would the feel of your body against me hurt, sweetheart. I only wish my conscience would allow me to take you to my bed tonight."

With a gentle hug he left her inside the entrance of her home. Lips brushing her forehead, he whispered huskily, "Later today, *mia cara*, we'll have a serious discussion about you becoming my permanent bed partner. A pleasure that can't arrive too soon for me."

"Umm . . . me too." Still drowsy, bemused by her day in Nick's company, Carlyn mumbled incoherently as the door latched behind her. As if in a dream, she walked up the stairs into the elegant bedroom and automatically prepared for bed. With a contented sigh she eased her weary body between the sheets.

Silvery hair in disarray, tumbling about her face to form a vivid halo, she drifted into a deep, dreamless sleep.

CHAPTER SEVEN

Carlyn groped awkwardly in the dim room for the ringing phone and woke the instant she heard Nick's deep voice. Checking the clock, she asked with concern, "Is anything wrong, Nick, it's only six?"

"Yes, I know, honey," he answered, his voice troubled. "I'm sorry to wake you but I have to leave immediately for New York. My manager was admitted to the hospital last night and his frantic wife told me that during emergency surgery the doctors found his stomach was cancerous. He won't be able to return to work of course, and it will take a few days to get everything running smoothly again. I want to make certain he and his family have everything they need."

"Can I help in any way, Nick?" Carlyn asked sympathetically.

"No, sweetheart. I'm dressed, packed, and booked on a seven-thirty flight."

Her heart was despondent that Nick had to leave but she was filled with pride that he felt such obvious concern for his employee.

"I don't even have time to come kiss you good-bye. I hope to be gone only a couple of days and I might be too busy to even phone." His husky voice betraying his seriousness, he questioned, "If being my traveling companion and sleeping each night in my arms sounds as good to you as it does to me, be waiting for me, darling." Obviously rushed, he whispered, *"Arriverderci, mi amore."*

The sudden click of the receiver stopped Carlyn's explanation that she wouldn't be there, that she had to report to duty the following Wednesday. Before she could get to the front door, she heard the low hum of the Porsche as Nick sped toward the airport. Saying a silent prayer for his safe return, she returned to the bedroom.

Her thoughts on Nick's sudden departure, she was unable to sleep and she decided to end her vacation and return to her apartment. The Malibu mansion had lost all appeal the moment she knew Nick was not staying next door.

In an hour her suitcase was packed, used linens were in the hamper, Carlyn was dressed and seated at the kitchen table. Marianne had told her a maid came in each week to clean, so she was saved any household chores.

Pencil poised over a sheet of notepaper, she pushed back her tumbled hair, then wrote in her neat, feminine style:

Dearest Nick,
I find the thought of a day alone desolate and unbearable. Without you the beach holds no interest. I will cherish forever our meeting, darling.

After the way I responded to your touch, need you ask if I will travel with you and share your bed?

I am leaving you my unlisted phone number and address, as I have to return to work soon.

The thought of being your wife fills my heart with

107

love. Love I ache to give you. I will be counting the hours until you come to me.

Yours forever and always,
Carlyn

As she sealed the note in an envelope, along with her address and phone number, she could not help but be disappointed that her days with Nick at this romantic setting were over. She had come expecting to rest and enjoy the sun, but instead she had found love. Laying the door key on the table, she took a last look around, then gathered her things together and locked the doors. She knew she would never forget the happiness she had found on the beach at Malibu.

She put her suitcase in the back of her Volkswagen before hurrying up the stairs to Nick's door. There was no mail slot so she placed a small potted plant over the edge of the envelope and set it directly in front of the door so Nick would see it the instant he returned.

Unaware of storm clouds gathering in the darkening, turbulent skies across the horizon, she set off for home, thoughts completely on Nick. She arrived before noon and unpacked before relaxing in her favorite chair. Bare feet tucked under her, she scanned the accumulated mail without interest.

Feeling as if she'd burst if she kept the news about Nick to herself, she dialed Marianne. Without explanation she asked her to come over: she had something exciting to tell her.

Marianne arrived shortly, grumbling about the sudden change in the temperature as she searched Carlyn's face for clues to the tale she was anxious to hear.

Carlyn bent to give Billy an affectionate hug before reaching to see her niece as she lay in her mother's arms. Betsy gurgled with delight as her aunt gave her a noisy, teasing kiss.

"Can I get my toys, Aunt Lyn?" Billy asked, brown eyes eager.

"Of course, honey, you know where they are. You'll find a special surprise in there today."

As Billy rushed to the closet that contained his box of games and trucks, Carlyn knew he would be content to play quietly as she and Marianne talked.

"Bright of you to have a toy box," Marianne stated, setting her purse on the coffee table. "The greedy little beggar can hardly wait to see what you got him."

Billy opened the sack filled with sea treasures, then came rushing back to clamber onto the couch, his high young voice filled with excitement. "I love you, Aunt Lyn!" He reached upward to give her a wet kiss on the cheek. "Where did you get the shells? They smell all salty and funny. I'm going to show them to Daddy, then my friends and kindergarten teacher." He scrambled off the couch to rush back to his treasures, yelling thank you over his shoulder, not waiting for her to answer.

"You're welcome, honey." Carlyn laughed, smiling at his happy face. Then to her sister-in-law, "Let me hold Betsy, Marianne. There's some fresh-brewed coffee waiting for you in the kitchen." She cuddled the soft sweet-smelling body to her breast.

Marianne returned from the kitchen, sipping her coffee, and sat opposite Carlyn to wait for her to explain the call. "God, Carlyn, you should get married," she exclaimed, looking at the lovely sight of Carlyn gently holding her daughter. "You're the perfect picture of motherhood. Why don't you quit your job, find a man, and raise your own family?"

Carlyn's violet eyes sparkled with happiness as she blurted out wistfully, "That's my news." In a voice high with excitement she hurriedly told Marianne about meeting Nick, detailing everything but the intimate parts of their relationship. Breathless after her long speech, she was dismayed to see Marianne frown seriously.

"I thought you'd be happy for me. I love Nick so much, I can hardly bear it when we're apart for even a day."

"But, Carlyn!" Marianne cut her short. "You've only known him for five days! You've never shown much interest in forming a relationship before, and now all of a sudden you're in love with a man you've only known a matter of days. That's too quick. Has he asked you to be his wife?"

"Well, no . . . not exactly," Carlyn admitted. "While he's in New York, he wants me to make up my mind about traveling with him." She deliberately omitted his query about sleeping in his arms at night.

"Being married is not a necessity for traveling with a man," Marianne told her bluntly. "Did he ask you to sleep with him?"

Flushing at the pointed inquiry, Carlyn answered truthfully. "Yes, but it's not what you think. He loves me, Marianne. Nick is too fine a man to want only a casual relationship with me."

"You're trying to tell me," Marianne asked, relaxing in the armchair, "that he does not sleep with women he is not married to?"

Carlyn placed Betsy, who had fallen asleep, on the couch. She smoothed the baby's jumpsuit before looking up. "No, he has admitted to having numerous short-term relationships."

Violet eyes brimming with unshed tears, she exclaimed sadly, "I thought you would be pleased that I fell in love and all you do is make me sound foolish. You couldn't be more mistaken. Nick will return in a day or two, and soon as he comes to me, I'll have you and Bob come meet him. Then you'll see for yourselves how wonderful he is."

The memory of his urgent kisses and tender caressing hands brought a dreamy flush to her face as she whispered, "I never hoped to find a man who makes me feel as he does, Marianne."

"No doubt, if he's as handsome, rich, and experienced as you say, he's made many women feel the way you do!" Marianne retorted coolly. "Did you tell him you were a police officer?"

"No, not yet, but I will as soon as he returns, and he won't care. Wait until you meet him, please, before saying anything else. He's not like you say at all. Our love is really different. He told me I was . . . unlike any woman he had met before."

"Typical statement from a man on the way to the bedroom. On the way out though they often change their tune. He didn't seduce you, did he?" she queried worriedly as she noticed Carlyn's heightened color.

"No, but he could have. I would have given him anything he wanted. He was the one who always pulled away before we went too far."

"My God, you really do have it bad." She spoke over her shoulder, returning to the kitchen for another cup of coffee. "I can hardly wait now to meet this paragon of manhood. Sorry if I hurt you with my comments but I don't want to see you hurt. Five days with a man is not long enough to know how you'll feel for a lifetime. I know I encouraged you to have a lighthearted affair but this bit with Nick sounds heavy—too heavy to last, sweets!"

Disturbed by Carlyn's seriousness and anxious to confide the news to Bob, Marianne gathered Billy and Betsy, leaving after a brief hug. She told Carlyn to phone the minute Nick arrived.

That night, indifferently watching the late news on television, Carlyn saw film of a sudden low-pressure zone that moved in over the coast. The fierce storm that followed hit the southern California coast from Santa Barbara to San Diego. Heavy winds and high waves battered the shoreline, followed by a torrential rain. A freak storm, the weather forecaster called it, caused by turbulence from a Baja California hurricane.

Unprotected furniture on the deck in Malibu tumbled and rolled, knocking the potted plant over. Carlyn's letter, released from its weight of the pot, tossed in the air, over the stairs and across the walk, where it ended its flight on the side of the road. Rain completed the damage and the letter was soon soggy, neither legible nor available for Nick's scrutiny.

Carlyn reported back to duty, settling easily into the well-known routine of her job with the Los Angeles Police Department. She rushed home each evening, eager to hear from Nick, expecting the ring of the phone or a knock on the door.

Aware how busy Nick would be settling his business affairs in New York, she was unconcerned until the first weekend passed. Marianne phoned each day, inquiring if there was any news. Her suspicions about Nick's seriousness toward Carlyn began to take its toll on Carlyn's own confidence in his love.

Running slender fingers through her silky hair, Carlyn paced the living room. Nervous, unable to relax, she began to despair over the lack of contact with Nick as long days of silence continued unchanged. She sobbed softly, tears streaming down her face unchecked as she prayed that Nick would come to her and explain his absence.

Suddenly the piercing ring of the telephone cracked the silence, causing her nerves to jump. She rushed to the phone, her heart beating rapidly, and picked it up before the second ring.

"Sorry to disappoint you, but it's only me," Marianne replied sympathetically, noting Carlyn's dejected sigh when she recognized her sister-in-law's voice. "No need to ask if you've heard from Nick. What did you say in that note anyway?"

112

"I told him I loved him and wanted to be his wife," she cried sadly. "Deep in my heart I know he feels the same as I. He—he told me I was the other half of his heart."

"Okay." Marianne spoke consolingly. "It's obvious you can't go on another three weeks like this. Pick me up and we'll drive to Malibu and get things straightened out one way or another. Surely your lover is back from New York by now. I hate to keep discouraging you, but so far everything points to the fact that Nick's interest isn't as serious as yours. It's darn silly to keep tearing yourself apart waiting for him to phone."

Carlyn hung up the phone, trying hard to regain control of her emotions. The white jeans were loose around her waist as she fastened them over her violet print blouse. The sleepless nights and lack of appetite had taken their toll on her figure, though her lustrous hair gleamed with health as she tied it back with a silk scarf.

Within minutes she had arrived at her brother's home. Giving him and the children a fond hello, she hurried her sister-in-law out the door. Her mind was made up that Marianne's suggestion was surely sensible and she was anxious to be on her way to discover if it was true.

As she eased from the curb she felt Marianne's keen look.

"You look terrible, Carlyn. You've lost weight, your eyes are shadowed and despondent. I'm jealous though, as you appear even sexier with that mane of silver hair and voluptuous top half." Glancing down at her own small breasts, she laughed. "Oh well, at least I know Bob didn't marry me for my dimensions."

"Bob married you because he loves you," Carlyn assured her unnecessarily as she maneuvered her small car through the heavy traffic in Santa Monica.

Voice distraught, eyes shimmering with tears, Carlyn whispered, "You can't imagine how crushed I feel. Every

113

moment was perfect when we were together. It felt like destiny to meet Nick," she added with remorse.

"You, my sweet sister-in-law, are not the first nor the last to go through the throes of love. It happens to all of us—and usually many times. I had several distressing romances before I met your brother, and when each one was over, it seemed like the end of the world. All's not lost because Nick turned out to be a dud," Marianne blurted out without thought.

Carlyn's temper raised at the derogatory comments about Nick, and she snapped back. "All you've done right from the first is put Nick down. I refuse to hear one more word against him or about his transient feelings for me! I'm having a hard enough time driving in this busy rush-hour traffic as it is, so please be quiet."

"Okay!" Marianne retorted huffily. "I was trying to help by being realistic and letting you know you weren't the only one who has had problems with romance."

Ashamed of her outburst, Carlyn spoke softly. "Why don't you talk about the kids. A change of subject will help us both."

In good humor again Marianne spent the rest of the trip bragging about Betsy's progress in talking and Billy's genius in arithmetic, just like his daddy. She was proud of her children, and the time passed quickly as she related happy events of her days providing a loving home for Bob and their children. She was still talking when they arrived at the colony.

Carlyn's breath caught nervously in her throat as she was waved past the gate. She pulled to a stop in front of the house, unable to hide her bitter disappointment at not seeing Nick's Porsche. Without a word to Marianne she rushed from the car and up the stairs. Observant, she noticed the potted plant was in its normal place, proving beyond a doubt that Nick had been there.

She knew instinctively that Nick was not inside, but she

rang the bell anyway. The house had a vacant, forbidding look. She glanced beyond the deck railing; the distant ocean and tangy salt-laden air didn't register on her consciousness.

Her narrow shoulders slumped dejectedly at the pain of finding Nick had not contacted her. At the sound of the car door slamming she turned. "Come on up, Marianne. Nick's gone. He's been here though. The plant's been moved and my envelope's gone."

Tears falling freely down her face, she cried plaintively, "I—I can't bear to stay here any longer." She looked around for the last time, remembering so strongly the happiness she had felt. Nick's image was everywhere and she couldn't endure another minute's pain.

She fled down the stairs, slumped in the seat of her Volkswagen, and cried into her hands. With a broken voice she called to Marianne as she neared the car, "Hurry, please. I . . . want to go home. I'll ask the guard if he knows where Nick is, but I doubt if he can help me now either." Slender hand shaking, she wiped her tear-streaked face before starting the car and making a U-turn back to the entrance gate.

Eager to speak to the lovely girl, the guard stepped forward as she stopped. He remembered well her pleasant smile when she had visited the previous month. Friendly and nice, he thought, not like some of those ritzy snobs who lived here and figured because he worked for a living he didn't enjoy a word of praise, a wave of a hand, or a pleasant smile. He stood neat and proud in his spotless gray uniform. "Can I help you today, miss?" he asked, his keen eyes noticing her sad face and brimming eyes.

"Would you happen to know Mr. Nick Sandini who was staying down the road, and if so, when he will be returning?"

He easily remembered the dark-haired man and replied confidently, "Yes, I know the man. He was here a couple of weeks ago." With a hand on his chin he pondered a moment. "Seems now it was on Saturday. He wasn't here but an hour or less before he stopped by my gate in a furious mood. Didn't hardly look up, but I noticed his expression was violent. Told me never to have anything to do with women." His face crinkling with laughter, he went on. "I remember distinctly him saying they were all alike and never understood what a man meant. He tore out of here racing his Porsche like the devil himself was after him. I enjoyed seeing the two of you together and thought what a nice-looking couple you made. You so fair and all next to his deeply tanned good looks." Peering in at her, he smiled. "Sorry, that's all I can tell you. Hope it helped some."

Wretched at the news and the guard's revealing statements, Carlyn looked with shocked eyes at Marianne before thanking the man. Silent, she drove toward West Los Angeles.

Several miles passed before she felt calm enough to speak. "You were right after all. Nick was here two weeks ago and I've been home every night and no word from him. Last weekend I never left the apartment once for fear I'd miss his call. The painful part was his comment to the guard about women never understanding what a man means."

She gripped the steering wheel so tightly, her knuckles turned white. "I feel so ashamed. I told him I loved him and would marry him, and he only wanted a casual relationship." Her troubled voice filling the car, she spoke bitterly. "What's even worse is that the way I feel about Nick I'd quit my job and follow him to the end of the earth today if he would ask me. With or without marriage! I'm not the straitlaced prude you think I am, Marianne. My first lover makes me forget my parents' advice and my own moral principles."

Marianne was unable to console Carlyn: there was

nothing she could do but listen. For the rest of the ride she sat silent. She felt certain that if Carlyn had fallen in and out of love dozens of times like most young women she wouldn't feel so disconsolate at finding out Nick was a heel.

"Penny for your thoughts?" Carlyn questioned curiously, unaccustomed to Marianne being quiet.

"I was thinking what a heel Nick is and that I was right all along!" she blurted out brusquely. "Those overly handsome types that get to middle age without settling down generally only have quick seduction in mind. Believe me, love, no man could be around you and not want to have sex!" Her voice carrying the fury she felt, she exclaimed, "He thought you were a gorgeous body he could use then discard, and I wish to heck I could give that callous monster a piece of my mind!"

"Stop it, Marianne! Despite the fact that you are undoubtedly correct, I refuse to hear another word against Nick. I love him . . ." she cried brokenly. "Can't you understand that this has not changed the way that I feel!"

She stopped in front of Bob and Marianne's home, said a hurried good-bye and drove to her apartment. Marianne's concern and willingness to listen to confidences at any hour of the day or night were welcome balm to Carlyn's emotions, battered by Nick's perfidy.

All pretense at control left as Carlyn entered her apartment. She fled to her room, dropping to her knees beside the bed. With her tear-stricken face in the palms of her slender hands, she prayed to God for Nick to return to her.

Let Nick come back to me, Carlyn beseeched Him, her soft voice breaking with sadness. *Let him hold me close and tell me all my fears are unfounded. Let me hear his deep voice assure me he loves me, that we will never part again.*

Carlyn could not be termed overly devout, nevertheless

she still had a deep faith in a supreme being who watched over those who believed. Her heart broken, her faith bruised by Nick's deceptiveness, she rose from her knees, determined that the future was no longer in her hands alone.

She splashed cold water on her tearstained face and, temporarily refreshed, sat before her dressing mirror. Trying to avoid eye contact with her image, she brushed her silver hair in long, soothing strokes till it gleamed. *I may have lost Nick,* she thought, *but I still have my career. My Lord, what a terrible sacrifice to have to make,* she cried, the pain of his loss seeming more than she could bear despite realizing her fortune in having a financially secure job—and more importantly, a stimulating one. She resolved to call upon her strength of character and force herself out of her depression and into her work. Nick would be pushed into the recesses of her mind, and she would throw herself headfirst into studying for the upcoming sergeant's exam. She felt confident in her ability to secure the promotion, and the extra responsibility of the supervisory position would help erase the vivid memories of her first unfortunate love affair.

Stricken face pale, bruised eyes vulnerable, Carlyn glanced in the mirror, lowering her lashes at once. The sad droop of her slender shoulders belied the fact that her future would be as gratifying as she expected.

CHAPTER EIGHT

Immediately after returning to duty, Carlyn was ordered to report to Captain Jack Stinson, Administrative Vice. As she drove to Central Facilities headquarters in downtown Los Angeles, her mind ran curiously through a list of possible assignments. She had no idea what Captain Stinson expected of her, but that was one of the things she liked best about her job: each day was a challenge—one she felt qualified to meet. One of nearly two hundred women police officers, she had pride in her profession.

Carlyn remembered clearly her twenty weeks at the police academy in Elysian Park, where all police officers, both male and female, received the same extensive training. Over nine hundred hours of exacting study in community relations, communication, patrol procedure, penal code; physical fitness programs comparable to the armed services' boot camp; followed by extensive in-field assignments were all a necessary part of the grueling eighteen-month probationary period. With all this behind her, she felt she had the ability and confidence to handle herself well in any situation.

In his third-floor office Captain Stinson waited for Carlyn. A tall, lean man with steel-gray hair and piercing blue eyes, he sat behind his desk. His manner assured, he observed the men summoned by him earlier. As they greeted each other his sharp mind was contemplating the feasibility of his plan.

"Sit down, men," he ordered abruptly.

Lieutenant Tim Carlson and Sergeant Ralph Pasternik complied, anxious to hear the reason for their unexpected orders. Carlson, average height and build with a wide smile, thick wavy light brown hair, and light blue eyes, had an outgoing, gregarious personality and a reputation for being quite a ladies' man. Pasternik, his antithesis, looked like a rancher, with a big powerful body and huge hands, yet handsome with curly black hair and gray eyes.

Sergeant George Smith seated himself across from the other men. His pale complexion, soft brown eyes, and fringe of red hair on his balding head gave his round innocent face the look of a dreamer, but in fact his mind was sharp and alert. All three men were excellent police officers and completely dependable.

"I've received documented information that Benny Valouse will arrive at L.A.X. tonight at nineteen hundred hours and I want to brief you on the assignment before Officer Carlyn Thomas arrives."

Thumbing through a thick pile of papers on his desk, the captain looked up, his expression grim. "I want to hang this dirty bastard—and if my plan works, we have a chance of doing so. Valouse has been directly responsible for drug-trafficking millions of dollars worth of heroin and cocaine yearly, along with profitable interests in prostitution. Despite this he has never been convicted of a crime. Not even a traffic ticket!"

Talking as he glanced through the papers before him he told his men, "I've asked Officer Thomas to report to me. The success of my plan depends upon her assistance. Looking through her package, I can see why she was so

120

highly recommended. She's brilliant, graduated third in her class at the academy, personnel ratings all in the upper ten percent, but equally important is the fact that she is beautiful and has a striking figure."

"How well we know!" Lieutenant Carlson interrupted. "There's not an officer who works downtown who isn't aware of Carlyn. It's worth giving up a day off just to exchange a few words and be the recipient of her gorgeous smile," he added exaggeratedly.

Captain Stinson raised his palm to stop their conversation. "It's rumored that Valouse's mistress, Marie Hill, is getting edgy. A striking redhead, she is the key to our success if we are to put him behind bars. Marie knows the inner workings of his illegal dealings and can give us names, dates, and places. Unfortunately she also knows he wouldn't hesitate to waste her if she turned informant. Currently she's hanging tight to his side for her own safety." Scrutinizing his men, he spoke with emphasis. "Now this is where Thomas can help. Valouse has always had a roving eye for sexy blondes . . . the bustier the better."

Sergeant Smith interrupted the captain, looking at the other men for agreement. "You couldn't get anyone better than Carlyn then, Captain. She's really stacked and her hair is a kind of silvery color but she always wears it confined on her neck. In fact she has a pretty prudish reputation."

"I know!" Lieutenant Carlson grimaced. "She won't fool around at all. I tried it, and she turned me down flat. I checked around and I found she hardly ever dates police officers. Everyone adores her and she's got quite a sense of humor, but emotionally she's an iceberg. What a waste of merchandise." His emotions were aroused just by thinking of her beautiful figure and passionate mouth. His mind reeled at the thought of making love to her.

"Hell, I don't blame her for not going out with you, Tim," his permanent partner in Ad. Vice, Sergeant Pasternik, teased. "She probably heard about you from one of your ex-wives."

"Three now, isn't it?" Sergeant Smith, a longtime acquaintance working in Narcotics laughed.

Lieutenant Carlson was accustomed to being the butt of their teasing about his interest in women and constant marital problems, so he retorted bluntly, "Don't get on my back. You know as well as I do police officers have one of the highest rates of divorce of any occupation. It's damn hard for a man in blue to be true with such a variety to pick from."

"Let's face it, it's not only that women can't resist our uniforms, they can't wait to get their hands on a steady income and collect our retirement pay," Ralph commented cynically.

"That's enough horseplay, men," the captain interrupted. "I want each one of you to realize what we're up against. Valouse is no small-time hood and won't hesitate to see his cohorts and trusted bodyguards eliminate anyone who gets in his way. My plan is to set Carlson up in a suite at the Royal Hotel with Carlyn as his high-priced mistress."

His keen eyes observing Carlson, he told him seriously, "I want you to discreetly solicit her services as a prostitute to Pasternik and Smith. Your cover will be an ex-con swindler from the Midwest. Act cocky about your hold over Carlyn and you'll be noticed. Valouse's redhead is still good-looking but her life-style is beginning to take its toll and she looks hard. I'm hoping that Carlyn's face and figure will draw him like a magnet."

As the three men slouched casually, their appearance belied the fact they were listening intently, minds alert to the dangers of the assignment ahead.

"Thomas won't be able to carry her gun, so if she finds herself in a delicate situation, she'll have to use her quick mind to get out of it. If Valouse should tumble to our setup, she could be in serious trouble. He has a violent temper and vindictive nature. Your job is to get his mistress jealous or mad enough to come to us for protection while she spills her guts out about his felonious activities. The minute we have her in protective custody, your assignment ends."

His fists slammed down on the desk as he bellowed angrily, "I want this bastard behind bars! The countless lives he has ruined eat at my insides." His intelligent eyes locking with those of his men as he looked at each in turn, he spoke vehemently. "Be careful. There have been scores of police officers needlessly killed in Los Angeles while on duty, and I sure as hell want you men to make certain the first female police officer to die isn't on this assignment."

"You can count on us, Captain. None of us wants to die a hero—it won't be a hardship keeping our eyes on Carlyn," Tim spoke up seriously, before the captain interrupted to continue.

"Her father and I went through the academy together and became good friends through the years. A more honest police officer you never met. I didn't think he would ever get over the death of his young wife, and I guarantee he'd be in a hell of a shape if anything happened to his beloved daughter. He was never keen on her joining the department in the first place."

Changing the subject abruptly, he added, "I've just come from Parker Center and talked with the chief. He and his deputy chief are aware of the plans and give you their best, though they're not optimistic about the results, to say the least."

Captain Stinson explained to Smith and Pasternik that he wanted them to act as free-spending conventioneers who were to approach Carlson about hiring Carlyn's services, but most importantly to act as the decoy's protection.

"We should be so lucky!" both sergeants cried in unison.

Smiling at their comment, the captain leaned over his desk, hands clasped in front of him. "Whenever you need to pass on information to her or Carlson, you can go to her room without raising suspicion. As you know, the hotel is large, expensive, and has a first-class lounge and bar. This is no Western Avenue twenty-dollar-a-trick deal. The selling of Carlyn's favors will be done in such a manner that the regular hotel guests will never have the slightest hint. Valouse will pick up right away on what's happening and, if interested in Carlyn, act from that. His ego will keep him from wanting to pay for what he thinks she'll be glad to give him free."

His gaze went to Carlson and he shrugged. "I hope Valouse tries to bribe Carlyn into leaving you, but you'll have to play it by ear. He may look like a creep to us, but he's never had any trouble getting good-looking women to put up with his slime to get at the furs and diamonds he rewards them with." Hearing a knock on the door, the captain looked up. "That should be Thomas.

"Come in," Captain Stinson called, and rose from his chair as Carlyn entered the office. "I believe you know Lieutenant Carlson," he said, pointing in his direction, "and this is Sergeant George Smith from Narcotics and Sergeant Ralph Pasternik from Ad. Vice."

As she smiled at the men the captain knew instinctively that she would be perfect for the assignment. A shrewd intelligent man, he had learned through his work to make quick judgments and make them correctly. Motioning to the vacant chair, he commanded kindly, "Sit down, Thomas. I have a lot of information to give you and I want to get started right away. I've taken the liberty of having you assigned to me on loan for some undercover work. I can't stress strong enough to all of you that utmost secrecy is essential throughout this entire job. No one outside this

124

office and the chief is to know about this. That means wives, parents, friends, and lovers. Your safety as well as that of your partners could depend on it. Have I scared you away, Thomas?" he inquired, impressed by her calm, confident manner.

"No, of course not, Captain, but what part do I play?" she asked, sitting straight against the back of the chair, hands folded in her lap, as she listened attentively, her lovely face holding the rapt attention of his men.

Her ID photos didn't do her justice, the captain thought, admitting that his men were correct. She was stunningly beautiful, with a slender, voluptuous figure. He explained the assignment in detail, aware she was cognizant of the seriousness of her part in the situation.

At a crossroads in her personal life, Carlyn knew this was an ideal way of taking her mind off Nick. Well-trained, she felt capable of handling the responsibility of the task, giving total attention to the captain's words.

Intermittent contact with prostitutes in her work had given Carlyn the insight into acting her part with skill. *At least he wants me to play a high-class call girl,* she thought wryly, aware of the vast difference between that and a streetwalker—despite their being in the same illegal business.

She knew streetwalkers aggressively hustled tricks for long, tedious hours seven days a week, depending on volume for their earnings. Their greedy pimps never hesitated to punish them severely if dissatisfied with the amount of money procured. This constant threat of violence tended to keep all the girls in their stables, intimidated.

High-priced call girls were usually outstanding in looks, fashionably dressed, and intelligent conversationalists. She had observed them solicit in plush bars and exclusive nightclubs—although they usually worked through referred customers on an answering service—preferring to entertain their tricks discreetly in luxurious rooms.

Carlyn sighed with relief at her assigned identity. She would do anything asked of her as a police officer but had serious doubts that she could have acted convincingly blatant enough to approach Valouse in sleazy surroundings without arousing his suspicions.

The captain took in Carlyn's severe chignon and conservative, though attractive, dress and told her directly, "You will have to make changes in your hairstyle, makeup, and clothing. I want you to look as provocative as possible," at the same time telling her of a woman in Hollywood who could sell her anything she needed in that line.

Looking at her high, firm breasts, he remarked bluntly, "I would prefer you don't wear a brassiere, but that is up to you of course." He then told them that if there were no further questions they could leave, wind up their affairs at home, and report to him at 0800 hours. "Good luck to all of you. You'll need it," he added truthfully as he dismissed them.

Each sipping a cup of hot bitter coffee, they talked over their assignment, making plans for the next day. Their rooms had been reserved, cars rented, and credentials with false addresses made up. To simplify matters they agreed to use their own names. Each anxious to make his own arrangements, they parted.

With limited time for shopping Carlyn drove to Hollywood on the way home. A petite lady with bright red hair and kind brown eyes rushed forward as Carlyn entered the tiny plush shop.

Her keen eyes sizing up Carlyn's figure in a single glance, she told her the captain had already phoned and she had taken the liberty of selecting several pieces of apparel. "One of our more exotic dancers ordered several things from me but moved without picking them up." Holding up a dress, she glanced at Carlyn for approval.

At the manager's request Carlyn tried on several of the outfits. The clothes were made of fine materials and all sewn with care, though the necklines made Carlyn doubtful as she surveyed her image in the mirror.

"With your figure, my dear, it is a crime to hide it in the simple little dress you are wearing, although I realize you are working. In the evening you should wear softer, free-flowing styles with deep necklines that emphasize the beauty of your bosom."

Carlyn purchased several of the less-revealing, but equally sensual, styles at comparatively modest prices, then drove home. She dumped her packages on the couch, relieved that at least that much was accomplished. Having stripped to brief underwear and a short lounge robe, she curled in her favorite chair to phone her brother.

"Bob, I wanted you and Marianne to know I'll be out of town for a few days. Could you call Dad for me? I wouldn't want him to worry in case he tried to phone and couldn't get me. Give the kids a kiss and take care, favorite brother of mine." She chuckled softly when he reminded her he was her only brother and then wished her a nice time on her trip.

Within a short time Carlyn had phoned her hairdresser, dressed, and was relaxing in a chair as her long hair was being shaped and trimmed after washing. Brushed out, the new style framed her face in feathery curls before cascading over her shoulders in gleaming strands of molten silver. Her appearance was remarkably changed by the stylish cut. Heavy eyeshadow, deep violet lipstick, and a strong musky perfume would complete the transformation.

Dressed in a short baby-doll nightie after her bath, Carlyn sat in her comfortable velour chair, applying deep purple polish to her finger- and toenails. Waving her hands back and forth to dry them quickly, she knew it would be hard to get used to seeing something other than the pale pearly pink she normally wore.

As she packed her clothes she had a momentary feeling of unease, wondering when she would be returning and what would transpire in the interim. She had worked several undercover details before and they had all been routine, accomplished without difficulty or undue concern on her part.

She blamed her trepidation on Nick, knowing it was unlike her to be unusually concerned starting any assigned task. Ever since her mother's death at the hands of a drug-crazed teen-ager, it was Carlyn's ambition to do something to help end drug abuse. She knew that busting Benny Valouse would stop one of the major drug suppliers in the United States, so she pushed thoughts of Nick from her mind and concentrated all her effort on her assignment.

Eye-catching in a mauve print silk dress with a seductive thigh-high slit on the side, her spike-heeled sandals clicking loudly on the hard floor, she walked through the hall. Carlyn's many friends did a double take, barely recognizing her at first. Her silky hair hung in gleaming waves about her shoulders and framed her face, expertly made up with emphasis on her lovely eyes.

Her feminine curves were taut and firm, the dress snug over the high tilt of her breasts and narrow waist. The exposed length of leg drew all eyes from her rounded thigh to fine ankles.

The last to arrive, she was greeted with astounded looks followed instantly by whistles of appreciation. Tim found it impossible to take his eyes off her as they went over final details and backup strategy plans, his blood pounding with desire. Dressed in a shiny black suit, wide yellow-print tie, and white shoes, he was being teased unmercifully by Ralph and George.

"Actually," Carlyn laughed, eyes shining with mirth, "I agree with them. That tie is terrible. Looks like a Christmas present from a wife."

"How did you guess?" he said dryly. "Received after our divorce! I outrank you three insubordinates, so quit laughing. This expensive suit befits my image of a small-time hood," he informed them, preening before the laughing group. "I'm supposed to dress to attract attention." Staring with mock scorn at the two sergeants, he scolded, "You two with your black uniform shoes will be made a block away."

"We're not that stupid, Carlson. We've got our clothes in our lockers," Ralph told him. He turned to Carlyn, his gray eyes expressive with appreciation for her beauty. "You really did a good job, honey. The lieutenant wouldn't attract a single glance if he entered the hotel stark naked with you beside him. You look so damn gorgeous, if I didn't know the real you, I'd proposition you right now myself."

"Wouldn't do you any good," George scoffed at him. "She's supposed to be worth a thousand dollars, and that kind of bread you don't have! Quit drooling and let's get going."

Undaunted, Ralph quipped, "Do you think the L.A.P.D. Credit Union would loan me the money?" Shrugging his powerful shoulders, he exclaimed with resignation, "Probably consider it unwarranted."

"So would your wife, Sergeant," Carlyn teased, taking their good-natured bantering with the humorous intent that was meant.

George, leaning back in his chair, coffee cup dangling from his hand, changed the subject abruptly, explaining to Carlyn, "Pasternik and I are going to act as wealthy farmers from the fine state of Iowa, attending an agriculture machinery convention and not above wanting to partake of a few extracurricular activities. We're leaving ahead of you to settle in and look for some action. We'll play it by ear on approaching Carlson about soliciting you. The first day or so we'll probably lounge around the bar, flashing a few big bills about and keeping Valouse under tight surveillance."

"Don't forget all your big bills are department money and you have to keep an accurate expense account to show the captain," Tim reminded them unnecessarily. "If any regular bar patrons become aware and attempt to solicit Carlyn, I expect you two to interfere immediately—without blowing our cover."

Ralph and George agreed without question, then left to check out their rented car.

Carlyn and Tim, in their rented black Lincoln Continental, traveled the short distance to Hollywood quickly. "Are you nervous?" Tim asked sympathetically, having experienced the same instinctive apprehension beginning an assignment whose potential was hazardous. "Don't worry, honey, everything's going to be fine. You look very beautiful and worth a hell of a lot more than a thousand bucks a trick." His eyes lingered briefly on each delectable curve before he pulled into the hotel's circular entrance-way.

"Thanks a lot!" she retorted, eyes flashing with chagrin.

"My God, doll, that was meant as a compliment." Easing to a stop, he grinned at her. "This is it. Let's go get that damn bastard for the captain! I know I'm sure ready to give him hell."

The doorman, clad in his red and gold uniform, bent stiffly to open the passenger door. His eyes widened at the long glimpse of silken thigh exposed to his gaze deliberately by Carlyn as she began her act.

Her lashes fluttering, she gave him a wide smile before walking toward Tim with an exaggerated swing of her hips. Pleased with the attention Carlyn was receiving, Tim demanded arrogantly that his luggage be attended to without delay. With Carlyn hanging on to his arm he registered, prior to taking the elevator to the ninth floor.

Their bellboy stared intently at Carlyn as he placed their luggage in the bedrooms, waiting afterward for his tip. His smile broadened as Tim nonchalantly gave him a twenty-dollar bill.

"Unpack and put your bathing suit on. We'll go to the pool for a couple hours in hopes of seeing our man and his mistress. It will give us a chance to get our bearings and settle down a bit."

A large bedroom and bath each side of the lounge gave Carlyn the privacy she had hoped for. She felt naked looking in the full-length mirror after changing into her violet bikini. Tiny scraps of material held together by silver rings on each side of her hip and the center of her bra would not go unnoticed. She thought the matching opaque jacket gave her a modicum of security, unaware the open front drew attention to the deep cleavage exposed in the skimpy bra top and to the smooth skin of her long shapely legs. She fluffed her hair and applied a touch of glossy lipstick, darker eye shadow, and a spray of strong perfume. Stepping into low-heeled silver sandals, she slipped several silver bracelets over her wrist, then fastened a thin silver chain around her ankle.

Tim's breath caught in his throat when Carlyn entered the lounge. "My God, I'm absolutely stunned," he exclaimed harshly. His nostrils flared as he caught the scent of her heady perfume.

"We're on assignment, Lieutenant!" Carlyn chuckled to break his seriousness, searching through her bag for some dark sunglasses.

She was unconcerned by his personal remarks; she knew he was an intelligent, dedicated police officer, and would never bother her unless she showed the desire to reciprocate. All three men were well aware of their precarious positions.

"I wish to hell we weren't—and drop that 'Lieutenant' right now," he said, leading her toward the elevators. At the mezzanine level they walked out to the pool, Tim holding Carlyn's arms possessively. Dressed in white shorts and a loud print shirt, Tim passed easily for a tourist. His flamboyant personality and blatant actions were an ideal cover.

Seated on the padded lounge, Carlyn glanced at the artificial blue color of the water in the Olympic-size pool surrounded by a broad flagstone patio. The landscaping was lush and well cared for: palm trees towered at the back edge of the pool, the long slender trunks looking barely strong enough to hold the cluster of fronds crowning their tops.

Tim lay back after ordering drinks, his eyes narrowed as he observed each group thoroughly from under his lashes. Speaking under his breath, he whispered, "To your left against the wall is our man, sitting at a table. Beside him on a lounge is Marie and looking none to happy. Those three goons travel with him everywhere for protection. He's made many enemies through the years."

As Carlyn rose to straighten the cushion behind her back, Benny's gaze was drawn to her striking figure. Relaxing into a reclining position, she bent one leg at the knee, the sun glinting on the silver chain on her ankle. She was unaware of his stare.

Tim accepted their drinks from the waiter and turned back to Carlyn. "I like those jangling bracelets and ankle chain. They're an added attention-getter and appear to be very effective already."

Deliberately looking away from Benny, Carlyn ran her fingertip around the top of her frosty glass of orange juice as she listened to Tim's talk and watched his numerous hand gestures. George and Ralph sat across the pool, boldly staring at all the attractive women while keeping Benny under strict surveillance.

Tim trailed his finger over her slender arm. Leaning forward possessively, he told Carlyn he thought it was best they leave. "An hour is long enough for his first glimpse of your charms."

As she rose Tim took her arm and guided her toward the opposite entrance, deliberately passing Benny and his entourage.

His appearance casual, Tim's eyes never left Carlyn's face, his grip reassuring her with his own confidence as they walked by Benny. Trying hard not to shiver, Carlyn could feel the hooded eyes of Benny Valouse inspecting every inch of her exposed skin. The thought of him touching her made her stomach turn in repugnancy.

In their suite Tim told Carlyn to relax, aware of her thoughts. Their plan had been set in motion and he felt it best to stay out of sight until dinner. George and Ralph would keep them posted on Benny's location throughout the afternoon.

"You did fine," he said, soothing her. "Although I could feel you falter for a second when we passed by his table."

"I know." She shuddered, noticing Tim's frown. "The thought of him looking at me and the life he leads made me feel sick."

"See that you get over that fast. You're supposed to encourage his interest, and if he sees your skin quiver at his glance or touch, he won't fall in with our plans. He's a clever, cunning man."

As Carlyn dressed for their evening in the lounge, George phoned to tell them Benny and his group were entering the restaurant.

Zipping her tight-waisted dress, Carlyn forced herself to relax, knowing she had to attempt to make contact with Benny that night. His cold, emotionless black eyes had filled her with revulsion as they slid over her figure when she walked by.

With grim determination she arranged her hair about her shoulders, added purple lipstick to her well-shaped lips, and, holding her breath, sprayed the erotic-smelling perfume to her wrists and throat. Her shoulders straightened before walking out.

On the way to the dining room Tim was awed by Carlyn's sophistication, finding it hard to believe how reticent her true personality was toward the many advances from her male co-workers. "You'll knock everyone speechless when you enter the dining room, Carlyn, I've never seen a more beautiful woman in my life."

"Thanks, Tim, but it's only the outer covering that attracts you. Inside I'm the same Carlyn," she teased, giving him a shattering smile before lowering her lashes over deep violet eyes.

Her hand resting on his arm, they waited for the maître d'hôtel at the entrance to the dining room. Her black dress glittered with sequins as she stood in the foyer, one enticing pale shoulder bared. A long side slit exposed the curve of her thigh when she moved. Silvery hair glistening in the dim light, all eyes were drawn to her tall regal figure displayed so provocatively as she walked gracefully on spike-heeled sandals to their waiting table.

She let her glance survey the room beneath the thickness of her lowered lashes, observing George and Ralph sitting unobtrusively in the far corner as they ate their dinner.

The dining room was elegant, with spotless white tablecloths, silver cutlery, and sparkling crystal. Each table held a single red rosebud in a slender crystal vase. She touched the rose with her finger, thinking how similar they were at that moment. *We're only for show, beautiful to look at, but not true to our nature.* The rose had no odor, unlike the sweet-smelling roses her mother had grown. Her beauty was breathtaking in the dimly lit room as she scanned the full menu. The diners would truly be stunned to know she was a police officer.

"It looks like the captain was right," George observed as he sliced through his tender steak. "The bastard hasn't taken his eyes off Carlyn since she entered the dining room—and his mistress is definitely not pleased by the lack of attention."

The two sergeants watched as Marie spoke to Benny in an attempt to divert his attention with her own charms. They relaxed, satisfied, as Benny gestured angrily to leave him be, his actions easily discernible across the width of the room. Subdued, Marie sat back, remaining silent during the rest of their meal.

Deliberately lingering over their coffee, they watched Benny and his group follow Tim and Carlyn to the lounge at the completion of their leisurely meal.

The seductive beat of the three-piece combo resounded through the darkened lounge as Tim and Carlyn danced rhythmically. Tim's practiced guidance and dry sense of humor caused Carlyn's soft laughter to occasionally rise above the pulsating noise.

Benny's hooded, reptilian eyes never left her figure as she appeared to dance with abandon, not realizing his every move was being watched closely by the four undercover police officers assigned to ensnare him in their carefully worked-out plan.

CHAPTER NINE

Conscious of Benny's intrigue with Carlyn, Tim placed his hand on her bare shoulder and led her to the bar. He sat down a few seats away from Benny, then ordered drinks, his resounding voice bragging to the bartender about Carlyn's beauty and talent. Impressed by his lavish tips, the bartender listened attentively as Tim boasted that they would be in Hollywood for a few days and would enjoy a little action.

Carlyn gave the bartender a slow, intimate smile, her lips parted and soft, her violet eyes shining with invitation, as he let his avid glance roam over her. Her eyes flickered as Ralph wrapped his long legs around a stool at her side.

Not showing the least sign of recognition, she turned her head as he asked if he could buy her another drink. "You'll have to ask my man, but if it's okay with him, I'm game." She leaned against his broad shoulder suggestively. "I've always been partial to big brawny men with curly dark hair."

Cutting short his conversation with the bartender, Tim moved behind Carlyn to confer in a low voice with Ralph. Ralph let his eyes slowly roam Carlyn's entire body as she leaned indolently against the bar, crossing one satin-smooth leg with exposed thigh over the other. Eyes darkening, expression interested, Ralph took out his wallet, and counted his money carefully before glancing back to Tim who stood smugly leaning on the bar.

The transaction went unobserved by the other patrons, but Benny Valouse was aware the instant it transpired and watched as the three left the bar, walking toward the elevators, Carlyn's waist tightly held in Ralph's strong clasp.

In the double suite Tim and Ralph switched on the television set. Immediately becoming immersed in a rerun adventure of Jack Lord in *Hawaii Five-O,* they were unconcerned that their own assignment was more daring than the one they were watching.

His eyes raised during a commercial break, Tim said that he and Ralph would stay there for an hour or so before returning to the bar. They would watch Benny closely, and if there was anything to report, George would come to the suite as if he too were a trick.

No longer needed, Carlyn wished the engrossed men a hasty good-night and retired to her room. After locking the door, she stripped and took a long hot shower to cleanse her body of the makeup, musky perfume, and most of all, the feeling of filth that acting the part of a prostitute gave her. The needle-sharp spray against her tender skin acted as a balm to her tightened nerves.

Carlyn tried for hours to get interested in a novel, but she finally gave up. Her mind was filled with thoughts of Nick as she lay in the darkened room. She could hear the husky timbre of his seductive voice, the touch of his lean, tanned hands, the exciting feel of his lips as their bodies entwined on the fur rug. As the sun began to rise, its light glimmering through her windows, she finally drifted off to sleep, remembering the pungent smell of burning eucalyptus logs while Nick caressed her responsive body. Tears dampened the sterile hotel pillowcase as she slept.

In the middle of a fitful dream she turned, her eyes fluttering until she focused on her travel clock on the nightstand. Ten o'clock. Suddenly she remembered she was supposed to join Tim for breakfast at ten. She bounded out of bed and tugged the swimsuit bikini panties over her narrow hips. In front of the mirror she adjusted the skimpy bra, hoping to cover as much as possible of her high, firm breasts before leaving her room. She brushed her hair high off her nape and fastened it with a silver filigree clasp pulling feathery curls around her ears and forehead. The upswept style emphasized her enticing profile and slender neck.

As they ate a late breakfast in their hotel room, Carlyn suggested to Tim that Benny might be more apt to approach if she was alone. Her eyes slightly shadowed from a restless night she pleaded convincingly, "Ralph told me Benny's mistress has a one-o'clock appointment with the hairdresser. That should take at least two hours. If he comes to the patio alone, I might be able to attract his attention and make our first contact."

"Sounds like an excellent idea," Tim agreed readily. "I'll hang around the bar after I get you seated in a lounge. That way I'll be close by if you need me."

Shortly after noon they entered the crowded pool area. Carlyn settled in a shaded lounge chair, before Tim left for the bar.

Leaning back, Carlyn stretched her body lazily on the comfortable cushion, enjoying the taste of fresh-made limeade, the frosty glass absorbing the heat of her nervous palms. A pair of large square-framed sunglasses hid her eyes. She realized how much she missed the security of Tim's presence as she waited alone.

The overhead sun danced over the surface of the glittering pool despite the filtering effect of her glasses. The smell of heavily chlorinated water filled her nostrils when an overly boisterous swimmer splashed it onto the flagstone. Waiting uneasily, she admired the skill of a lone diver as he arced his body through the warm dry air, entering smooth and straight with barely a ripple disturbing the surface. Envious of his freedom, she began to feel a sense of discomfort at the open invitations and interest she was receiving from unattached men.

She glanced at her watch. It had been over an hour and there was no sign of him. She decided to leave. Setting her empty glass on the patio table, she leaned over to retrieve her large canvas purse. The sound of a heavy body sinking into the adjoining lounge startled her. With a wary glance she looked straight into the black emotionless eyes of Benny Valouse.

He motioned curtly for his bodyguards to leave. "Well now"—he leered at her, letting his hooded eyes linger on the thrust of her full breasts—"I'm surprised to find you alone." His glance covered her body like a dirty hand, while they exchanged introductions.

Cringing inside, Carlyn forced herself to smile provocatively. Running her hand up the nape of her neck she lowered her lashes, visible beneath the smoke-colored lenses of her glasses. "My man prefers the bar to my company this afternoon," she said, pouting.

"Then he's a damned fool," Benny replied, his husky, guttural voice grating on her sensitive nerves. "He's too young to take care of all your . . . er . . . talents." His meaning was obvious as he continued to eye her curves suggestively.

Shrugging her shoulders, Carlyn retorted dryly, "Actually it's more like I take care of him." Her mind thinking quickly, she spent the next half hour satisfying his astute curiosity about her life and arousing his interest in her sexual proficiency.

Benny crossed his hands over his thick paunch, shutting

his eyes to the glare of the pool and the sun. "It's time to change men, baby. You shouldn't have to waste your looks hustling wealthy hotel guests to supply your man with drinking money."

"What do you think I am?" Carlyn asked indignantly. Having parried his questions shrewdly so far, she was aware of the necessity of replying correctly.

His eyes opened, pinning her with a cold look. "I know what you are! I watched you and your cheap pimp hustle that trick last night, which don't impress me. What does make an impact is your smooth, unblemished skin and sexy body." Leaning toward her, he took a short stubby finger and trailed it the length of her leg from calf to upper thigh. "Your erotic dancing made my blood run hot last night."

Carlyn's heart pounded, but she forced herself to stay motionless beneath the evil touch of Benny's hand, her body still as she smiled petulantly. "Your redhead doesn't look like she'd want to turn a duet into a ménage à trois."

"Fancy words for a threesome, baby, which is none of your damn business. Marie's greedy, mercenary soul will be satisfied when she goes." He took her right hand in his moist grip and pulled it to his full lips. His warm mouth moved against her palm as he waited to see if she showed any sign of rejection to his caress. Holding her hand away, he stared at it. "It would look better with an expensive diamond, don't you think?" The coarse black hair on his hands and wrists were abrasive to her tender skin. The scent of his cologne invading her nostrils was an odor she knew she would never forget in a lifetime.

Nerves screaming, she thought longingly of Nick's well-shaped hands, his tanned fingers with their gentle caressing motions stroking her body tenderly. *Oh Nick,* she cried. *What went wrong? It's unbearable to believe that the love we shared could end as swift as it began. I can't believe*

140

it's all in the past. Jarred into the present by Benny's harsh voice, she lowered her lashes, saying coyly, "Diamonds are always thrilling, but I can't see Tim losing me without protest."

"He won't utter a single complaint after my boys explain the situation, believe me, baby." Benny's breath fanned her face as he leaned closer, bragging arrogantly, "A night with me and no other man will ever satisfy you. I can be insatiable when a body arouses me like yours does. You really turn me on dressed in your skimpy bikini."

Carlyn hesitated, momentarily uneasy at the speed of her success in attracting Benny's interest. Giving him a wide smile, with lips parted and soft, she told him matter-of-factly, "I'll need a couple days to get my things together." That should be enough time for George and Ralph to approach Marie.

"Okay, but only because a sudden problem came up. In two days I return East and I expect you to accompany me. My boys will talk to your man tonight. Another thing—no more hustling tricks. If you're as good in bed as you look, the two-day rest will do you good." Stroking her naked thigh, he whispered, "Save it for me, baby . . . all of it!"

Images of Benny's mouth plundering hers, his naked body pressing against hers, flooded her mind and turned her stomach with revulsion. Before she flinched from him, Carlyn knew she had to get away. She excused herself, telling him she had to go to her suite. Her last glimpse was of him staring at her with a smile of satisfaction on his face, eyes cold and hard, still untouched by emotion, watching the curve of her buttocks and long slender legs. Forcing herself to walk seductively, she swung her hips slightly as she left the patio.

Once out of his sight she fled to the elevator and her suite. In the bathroom dry heaves racked her body as she leaned over the sink. Her brow beaded with perspiration, she splashed cool reviving water on her pale face. Returning to the sitting room, she sank onto the couch, her body trembling with relief at being alone.

Tim entered the room, concerned by her ashen face. "Feel pretty bad now, don't you? All three of us were watching you closely. He's interested for sure. It was all we could do to keep away when he put his filthy hands on your leg and held your hand. Did he seem suspicious?" Anxious to get an indictment, he was all business again.

"Not in the least. He told me a problem came up and he leaves for the East in two days." After a deep breath Carlyn excused herself to take a bath and change into more suitable clothing. "I have to wash the feel of his filthy hands from my body."

"I don't blame you, honey," Tim said sympathetically. "I want to let Intelligence know that Benny will be leaving. They can get in touch with New York and Chicago to see if anything of interest is happening there. Your information could be very helpful, you know."

Noticing a glazed expression on Carlyn's face, he queried, "What's the matter? I should think you'd be pleased with your work."

"He wants me to be his mistress, Tim. I agreed—if I could have the two days alone before leaving with him." She rose but stopped at the bedroom door. "His bodyguards are going to talk to you tonight."

"My God, you really went to work on him. The captain will be astounded at your success." A frown crossed his brow as he paced the floor, hands thrust deep in his slack pockets.

"What's the matter with *you* now? Aren't *you* pleased?" she asked curiously.

"Yes and no." Tim voiced his doubts. "It's going to be hard to work out anything with his mistress this quick.

Two days isn't enough time to handle things with certainty. The fact that we'll be rushed leaves more chance for something to go wrong, more of a gamble that we could forget something important."

He stopped to stare at her. "Everything would be perfect if he wasn't leaving so quick. We'll see what the captain advises. In any case you'd better hang close to the room for the rest of the day."

Carlyn watched with admiration as Tim's shrewd mind contemplated the possibilities that confronted them due to Benny's sudden departure.

Rubbing the back of his neck to ease the tension, Tim spoke. "After dinner we'll go to the bar, then I'll leave you for a short while so his goons can approach me easily." He smiled with pity. Maybe this was all too much for her. "I'm sorry, honey. Go take your hot bath and relax. I'll handle everything for a while."

Grateful to be alone. Carlyn tore off her bikini and soaked in scented water after briskly scrubbing her body over and over until satisfied in her mind that she had removed all traces of Benny's clammy hands from her thigh and moist mouth from her palm.

The solitude did her good; she felt rested and confident to play her part now. She looked through her new wardrobe and selected a bright purple two-piece silk pajama suit. Clad in brief lavender lace bikini panties and low-cut scalloped matching bra with tiny front fastener, her body was a smooth pale gold beneath the light.

The narrow silver belt that she tightened around her waist over the sleeveless hip-length top shimmered as it caught the shaded bedroom light. Her eye was drawn to the neckline that plunged enticingly over the rounded swell of her creamy breasts. The pajama legs were wide, the material flowing sensuously from the elastic waistband.

Her hair fell in thick waves around her face and shoulders, glinting equal to the fire reflected in her silver necklace. The darker eyeshadow deepened the color of her eyes to a dark velvety violet. The fragrance of her perfume was arousing as she walked into the sitting room. "Hi, Tim." And then noticing George and Ralph, "I didn't realize you were here."

Brows drawn together, George frowned with concern over the new development. "Tim told us about your remarkable success, yet I can't help but share his doubts." His intelligent brown eyes somehow looked out of place in his round childlike face. "But I think we should replan our strategy and proceed."

Ralph, dwarfing the lounge chair with his bulk, watched Carlyn as she walked to the window overlooking the Hollywood hills. She smiled over her shoulder at him as he complimented her. "Benny seems as stunned by your beauty as I am. I agree with George: I think we should go ahead. We can contact Marie tomorrow night. We think she'll be so wrathful about you replacing her, she'll testify without a qualm."

George walked to Carlyn's side. He placed his hand on her shoulder, patting it sympathetically. "The way I see it, if we can get through the next two days, you should be sleeping safe and sound in your own bed the evening after. How's that sound, honey?"

"Absolutely fantastic! I admit I'm not fond of playing a prostitute and Benny Valouse fills me with revulsion." Her stomach muscles tightened as she picked up her evening purse. The hours ahead would be crucial if their plan was to succeed. Tim's unusual silence since she had been in the room worried her. "What's the matter, Tim?"

His thoughtful eyes locked with hers as he shrugged nonchalantly. "Don't know actually. I have a bad feeling deep in my gut that things have gone too easy so far and aren't going to continue the same." Admiring Carlyn's exquisite face and innocent beauty, he blurted out, voice filled with fury, "Damn that Valouse! It's a violation of the pure-foods act for that bastard to even think of going to bed with you!"

Straightening his broad frame, Ralph smoothed his curly hair as he prepared to leave the room. "I agree, but don't worry about our assignment, Carlson. If we come against any problems, we end it. No sweat either way. Valouse continues on with his dirty business none the wiser and we bust him on his next trip to L.A."

George agreed with his partner, following him out the door. The two went to the dining room, slipping unseen from the suite.

After giving their partners ample time to be seated, Carlyn and Tim walked to the dining room, her appearance again noted by the diners. She swept gracefully by the tables, chin raised haughtily, eyes on the back of the maître d'hôtel, who seated her with a flourish.

Her glance spotted Benny instantly, and she smiled seductively, lowering her head to hide the revulsion at her deceit. He sat alone; his black formal suit, ruffled white shirt, and glittering diamond rings that adorned both small fingers did not go unnoticed by several attracted women. His ease in the elegant surroundings and expensive clothing helped overcome his unattractive stocky physique and cold black eyes, and the women boldly tried to catch his glance.

Tim's nudge brought her attention to the front of the dining room in time to see Marie stride in, slender figure covered in a full-length mink coat, the soft fur a vibrant mahogany-brown. She stopped for a brief instant beside their table, her green eyes flashing hatred at Carlyn, before walking toward Benny's table.

They watched as she lay her hand on Benny's shoulder

and bent to kiss him on the cheek. Rudely removing her hand, he shoved her roughly away. A sharp conversation was exchanged before she settled quietly, her expression brooding throughout their meal. There was little talk between them as they ate.

Carlyn lingered over her second cup of coffee, unable to eat her excellent meal with the thought of the inevitable contact with Benny ahead. Through lowered lashes she watched him rise and walk in her direction, Marie clinging to his arm possessively, his bodyguards following close behind.

He stopped in front of their table, his eyes for the first time showing emotion as he looked over Carlyn's bare arms and deeply veed blouse. They glittered a deep ebony with lust for her body. His arrogant stance revealed his confidence in his ability to command and coerce. It showed in his defiance of law-enforcement officials, and in the brutal, emotionless governing of his drug-pedaling empire. His eyes glittered as they locked with Carlyn's. "Meet me in the bar later," he commanded bluntly, before turning to Tim and adding insolently, "Alone!"

Tim blustered purposely. "The two of us will be glad to join you later. All private arrangements are made through me." Tim threw his shoulders back and returned his dismissing gaze unperturbed.

"I'll see her alone! You'll see my boys," Benny growled back.

Both Tim and Carlyn noticed the enraged expression on Marie's face. Her patience had run short; she was incensed by Benny's attention to Carlyn. Cautiously she placed her hand on his arm. Aware of his violent temper and coolness toward her since arriving in Hollywood, she purred sweetly, "Benny honey, can't we go to our room now?" His head nodded in agreement, and they left, Marie shooting a vehement glance at Carlyn as she walked away.

Hands clasped before him on the table, Tim frowned. "There goes that old gut feeling again. His mistress abhors you. Her behavior borders on hysteria, and nothing can foul up a smooth operation more than an emotionally unstable female."

Taking no offense at his criticism of her sex, Carlyn agreed that her animosity was intense. "Benny must have told her about me."

"Obviously. We'll take one thing at a time, and one way or another we'll soon find out if the captain's plan works." Helping her from the table, Tim held her hand a moment, whispering, "Let's go to the bar and see what he has in mind for me. I know damn well what he has in mind for you. He was practically eating you with his eyes, the dirty, slimy bastard! Did you notice all the women giving him the eye when they spotted his twin set of five-carat rocks!"

In the vacant foyer Carlyn added fervently, "Yes, and both purchased with dirty money. By the time his money is laundered, it's far removed from the addicts eating their insides out on his supply of drugs. All of them willing to sell their souls for the price of a fix."

Tim's concern for law and order flowed through his bloodstream. "Same goes for prostitution. Treating girls like cattle, shipping them from one area to the next when they get too familiar with the local vice officers—yet the bastards behind it all get by with it year after—"

"Sh, Tim, here come some people," Carlyn interrupted his fervent scorn. Quickly slipping his arm around her waist, he told her a joke on the way to the bar, certain that none of his comments were heard. Carlyn chuckled at his ridiculous wit as she climbed on the tall barstool.

George and Ralph were good-naturedly arguing at the end of the bar as they sipped cool glasses of foamy beer.

Benny, followed by his three bodyguards, entered the lounge, seen approaching them through the broad bar mirror. Carlyn forced a welcoming smile as he seated himself on the stool beside her.

Both elbows resting on the padded bar edge, Benny let his eyes roam over her body, lingering on the fullness of her breasts. He took her hand and gripped it tightly, his strength surprising Carlyn.

He's like a bull, she thought, moistening her suddenly dry lips with the tip of her tongue. She knew she had made an error when she thought he would be soft and weak. She had underestimated his power, a mistake she shouldn't have made.

Motioning to Tim with his hand, he ordered abruptly, "Go talk with my boys. I'll take care of your woman, understand?" One of his men stepped forward and grabbed Tim's elbow to escort him to a dark corner table, as Ralph and George observed their move unnoticed.

Benny leaned sideways, his stubby hand clasping Carlyn's waist. Kneading the soft flesh intimately, he pulled her close. As he bent his head to her face his liquored breath filled her with repugnance.

Aware of her nervous glance as she watched Tim, he demanded that she look at him. The sight of her creamy breasts in the clinging silk made him shudder. "My God, baby, you're really built. My hands are aching to grab you right here and now."

He raised her hand, rubbing the palm with his thumb, his diamond ring flashing fire. Carlyn felt revolted but, playing her part, flashed a wide smile.

"Come to my room tomorrow noon," Benny ordered. He drew her palm to his mouth and circled it with his tongue, his ebony eyes filled with lust. "A couple of hours is long enough to see if your experience matches your looks." His guttural voice at her ear, he bragged, "By the time I'm satisfied, you'll be like the others, begging for more!" Aroused by her nearness and her perfume, he groped for her lips.

No, I can't let him kiss me, she thought frantically. Quickly, she twisted to avoid contact with his mouth, her glance turned toward the lounge entrance. Her inner cry was for her assignment—and her agony—to come to a swift, successful conclusion.

CHAPTER TEN

Face ashen, eyes wide with disbelief, Carlyn's heart lurched in horror as she spotted a tall familiar figure at the doorway. *It can't be,* she thought, aghast. She stared at Nick, unconsciously pulling her hand from Benny's to clasp her wineglass. Her knuckles clenched, their grip threatening to break the fragile stem. *Dear God, help me please,* she prayed silently.

Confused and hurt that Nick had failed to contact her, she recalled the power of his hard, sensuous body and her uninhibited declaration of love in the note she left him at Malibu. *Oh, Nick, how smug you would feel to know I love you even more now,* she wept inwardly. She watched him hesitate briefly. He was so virile, still devastatingly handsome, a bit leaner, his face taut, his exciting mouth held in a thin line. The fabric of his black evening suit stretched taut across his broad shoulders as he walked lithely to a seat at the bar. His hand raised, motioning to the bartender for service.

Carlyn trembled with terror when he ordered a drink and casually glanced around. Indifferent to his surroundings, he nonchalantly looked over the boisterous group of sophisticated people enjoying their cocktails and listening to the seductive beat of a combo.

Stunned by the shock of his unforeseen appearance, she felt hypnotized, uncertain how to react. His interference was inescapable and would endanger their undercover work unless she immediately thought of a convincing explanation for her overt blatancy. With a shock she felt a hand slide the length of her bare arm to stroke her waist. Nick's startling emergence had made her momentarily oblivious of Benny's propinquity.

Carlyn watched Nick's head turn her way, a soft poignant moan of helplessness escaping her parted lips. Her silvery hair shone like a beacon in the dimly lit lounge, drawing his attention. His eyes narrowed, his expression turning savage as he scrutinized her carefully. Disbelieving, he saw Benny's head intimately descend toward her shoulder.

Obtuse to Carlyn's dilemma, Benny assumed she was sensually stirred by his touch. Raising his lips from her neck, he was annoyed to see her gazing at an aristocratic-looking man across the bar.

Nick's untouched drink sloshed the counter as he slammed it down carelessly. He strode toward Carlyn, stopping with his long legs braced and tanned fists clenched in anger. As he stared at her intently, his eyes darkened with fury. "Get rid of him!" he commanded hoarsely. "I want to talk to you privately." Grabbing Benny's arms, Nick roughly jerked them from Carlyn's body, incensed that she dared to let another man touch her.

Benny started to rise, infuriated that any man dare order him to leave, had the nerve to touch him in a brutal manner. His face reddened, expression bellicose, as he tried to attract his bodyguards, still engrossed with Tim.

Aware of Benny's murderous rage, Carlyn knew that Nick's safety depended on her imminent actions. Hurried-

ly she devised a plan, then proceeded with the most agonizing part yet of her scam.

She leaned seductively against the back of the bar.
Calmly crossing her shapely legs, she deliberately arched
her back to let Nick see the deep vee of her plunging
neckline. Her stare was aloof, violet eyes bold and uncaring as she spoke in a hard voice. "Hello, Nick. I didn't
think I'd ever see you again."

Nick's expression changed to revulsion as Carlyn
draped her slender arm around Benny's back, her head
leaning against his bull-like shoulder. Silvery strands of
her stylish-cut hair glimmered in startling contrast against
Benny's black jacket as she introduced them. "I'd like you
to meet Benny Valouse, a very good and . . . very personal
friend. Benny, this is Nick—Sandini, isn't it?—a casual
aquaintance from my past."

Enraged, Nick burst out, "Who the hell is this fat bastard?"

One of the bodyguards, spotting his boss's glance,
walked toward the bar. Confident with the approach of his
own man, Benny rasped, "Move on, Sandini, and be
damned glad you called me a bastard in this busy lounge.
No one speaks to me like that and gets away with it," he
threatened seriously. "If you're a past customer, I'm sure
you got your money's worth. As of now her services are
no longer for sale."

Interrupting, Nick growled with anger. "I don't know
what's going on here, but believe me I intend to find out."
Stunned by Benny's reference to Carlyn's past life, Nick's
eyes locked with hers in a vain attempt to force an explanation about her drastic change of character.

A brief side glance warned Carlyn that Nick was in
immediate danger as she noticed the bodyguard approach.
"Get lost, Nick," she blurted out abruptly. "I don't have
time for anyone else now that I've found the type of man
I've been looking for all my life." Leaning back toward

Benny, she cupped his face in her hands, placing her darkened, glossy lips for an agonizing second on his moist, seeking mouth. "Isn't that right, Benny sweetie?" she asked, her voice lowering to a sensuous whisper.

Dazed by Carlyn's actions, Nick paled. He shot her a last look of incredulity as he spun around and strode rapidly from the lounge, his back held ramrod straight with the force of his anger.

I've lost Nick forever now, Carlyn thought sadly, barely able to hold back a cry of pain as she watched him leave. Breaking contact with Benny, she swiveled forward, hands playing nervously with the stem of her glass. With grim resolution she forced herself to play out her part in the surreptitious drama until the end.

Benny bent to touch her, his hand sliding up her bare arm. "Who was he?" he suddenly demanded. "An unsatisfied customer?"

"You could call him that," Carlyn replied woodenly. Her control threatened by the traumatic confrontation with Nick, she asked Benny to excuse her for the rest of the evening. "I have a headache and want to feel good for our . . . preflight party," she lied, squeezing his hand in an attempt to assure him of her sincerity.

"Fine, baby. I want to talk with Carlson anyway." His breath fanned her sensitive skin as he pressed his lips against her alluring shoulder. "Room six-oh-nine, twelve noon sharp!" With a smug expression exuding conceit about his sexual technique, he boasted, "I guarantee you'll prefer me to those young punks you've been bedding." His pitch-black eyes lingering lustfully on her voluptuous figure, he added a final remark. "I can assure you, baby, this Hollywood visit will be one you'll never forget." His pudgy hand fondled her silk-clad thigh openly, the palm moist and clammy, as he anticipated the next day.

"I'll count the hours until noon," Carlyn purred softly.

It took her last bit of control to give him a wide seductive smile.

Anguish at seeing Nick overcame her as she slid from the stool. Her legs quivered, threatening to buckle as she walked from the lounge. In a daze, her vision was blurred by the trauma of facing Nick's wrath. Once she was alone in the elevator, she leaned against the paneled wall for support, arms crossed over her stomach in sudden pain. She knew she had destroyed any chance of reconciliation with Nick, but he was in grave danger—she had acted in the only way possible to ensure his safety and that of her partners, who remained unaware of her predicament.

Until her assignment was ended by the captain or Tim, it was her sworn responsibility to continue with her official duties. Any personal loss was a risk she had to be prepared to bear. It was now imperative she explain to her partners what happened as soon as possible. If Nick gathered the slightest hint that she was lying and in danger, he wouldn't hesitate to take on Benny Valouse, his three henchmen, and the Los Angeles Police Department for giving her the assignment.

Her stomach lurched as the elevator stopped, its wide doors gliding open soundlessly. Desperate to get to the sanctuary of her room before collapsing, she rushed, head down, along the carpeted hallway. The shock of seeing Nick caused a sick feeling to spread throughout her trembling abdomen.

She was oblivious of the second elevator pulling to a stop and the tall dark man who stepped out, intent on the dejected figure fleeing before him. His palm muffled her startled cry as he grabbed her from the back, roughly pushing her into a suite several doors from her own.

She struggled and turned to see her attacker, prepared to defend herself. Nick! Her eyes took in the fury of his face as he released her.

He slammed the door shut, locked it, and placed the key

in his pocket, his narrowed eyes never leaving her white face. Like a predator with his quarry backed against the wall, Nick growled deep in his throat. "Now, sweetheart, start talking! Tell me what the hell is going on. For three weeks I've searched night and day for you, out of my mind with worry." His voice seethed with anger. "To find you impersonating a two-bit whore leaning against the arm of that fat creep is the biggest shock of my life!"

Wary, Carlyn stood in the center of his room, quivering chin held high, hands clenched at her sides, trying vainly to regain a modicum of self-control.

Eyes darkened to steely-gray, Nick berated her. "The thought of someone else's hands touching you, you placing your soft mouth on that bastard's lips, makes me want to heave." Moving forward, he held her unresisting body at arm's length, shaking her furiously with each harsh word spoken. "Are you so damn stupid that you can't recognize what type of slime he is? That man actually smells of crime and corruption!" Her thick feathered hair hung in enticing disarray about her shocked face when he stopped. His hands bit into her slender, drooping shoulders cruelly, like steel bands of torture.

Carlyn drew back. She ached to tell Nick the truth, that she loved him and only him, that she was aware even more than he, just how corrupt Benny was, but she knew it was impossible. Just one wrong word and Nick could blow her cover, endangering her partners. She had to disillusion him so completely that he would leave and never return.

Her eyes raised, filled with distaste, as she boldly held his glance. "I'm not the stupid one, Nick . . . you are if you fell for my innocent act on the sands at Malibu," she blurted out insolently. "For kicks I often enjoy duping some gullible stud into believing I'm a virgin! My God, it's been so long since I was innocent, I can't remember when I lost it!"

Hissing with contempt, she continued her taunting. "I

can't believe I so easily convinced an admitted womanizer that I was untouched." Carlyn's chin raised defiantly, her deep violet eyes glittering with the same allure as her parted lips. "Get out of my way, Nick. I never go into any man's room unless I've got a thousand bucks in cold hard cash stashed in the bottom of my purse."

Her sudden burst of harsh laughter was scornful as she plunged the final thrust. "You even had the nerve to think you taught me how to kiss. You're an amateur, Nick. I could teach you things that would curl your shiny black hair in knots."

"Teach me? I think not, witch, but we'll soon find out." He grabbed her and shook her with fury until her face paled and hot tears fell involuntarily from her haunting eyes. Surprised by her tears, Nick stopped, pulling her body tightly against the length of his own. His mouth took hers in a brutal, searing kiss. He unmercifully ground his hard teeth against her tender lips until she cried out in pain.

"Tears won't help you now!" Nick mocked brusquely, his mouth plundering hers again. "If it's money you want, I'll pay you well. It'll be a cheap lesson at twice your price." His grip was viselike as he spoke against her throat. "To think I've dreamed of the moment when you'd be my wife . . . wanted you for the mother of my children!"

Physically shocked by the anger of his words, the pain of his punishing hold, she cringed at the disgust visible on his hardened features. She remained silent, but her eyes sparked fire as she returned his stare.

Cupping her face, he laughed bitterly as he forced her to listen to his bitter tirade. "It's no wonder you were evasive about your job! Invited to a millionaire's home, knowing the owner casually but not his wife, your brother thinking your work dangerous and overpaid, only consorting with married men while working, having to be in good shape. Even pretending you'd never been French kissed—

'too intimate,' you told me coyly. Oh, yes, my lying witch," he sneered, "I remember every single word. No wonder you laugh at me. You knew damn well I ached to where I couldn't sleep at night after leaving you untouched."

His gaze slid over her smooth face, lingering on the beauty of each feature, the appeal of her lips swollen from his rough kisses. "Despite that revolting perfume and dark lipstick, you're still the most desirable woman I know." Shuddering, he warned her furiously, "I want you, Carlyn . . . innocent or not."

Groaning hungrily, his mouth clamped over hers. He kissed her savagely, without mercy. His hands gripped her shoulders with a terrifying need to punish. "The last laugh's mine, sweetheart. I'm going to take ruthlessly what I would have given with love from the first day we met."

Frightened, she gasped as he molded the hard contours of his aroused body to her, forcing her to feel his need. Each bitter word was a knife thrust through her heart, but she stood still, lips sealed.

"One time, sweetheart, will convince me how foolish I've been." His face buried in her hair, she heard his muffled voice moan, "I loved you, Carlyn, would have died happy in your arms, your body arched to mine in the culmination of our passion."

Oh, how I ached to hear those words, she cried with despair. The tears that streamed freely down her face now were no longer from physical pain. She shook her head in dispute of all his false accusations, feeling faint from outrage and shame.

His breath warm on her neck, she felt his mouth move over her skin as if he wanted to imprint the taste forever on his memory. He lifted her supple body into her arms, and strode across the sitting room to his luxurious bedroom. "Time to earn your money. Believe me, I intend to use every penny's worth!"

He threw her onto the bed, then pinned both her arms above her head as he leaned over her. "Show me how a professional does it, sweetheart. Back up your blatant claims! Teach me, witch . . . now!" His eyes glittered as he covered her body with his.

"No, Nick! No . . . !" she beseeched him, squirming wildly to break his viselike hold on her arms. Tears ran down her cheeks as she pleaded helplessly, "Not like this, please—" Her voice broke off as his pitiless mouth descended to her parted lips.

Incited by her furious struggles, he was ruthless, overpowering her with his strength as his mouth moved over her face to the vulnerable hollow of her neck. Her throat convulsed in pain at his harsh treatment. In one ruthless motion he grabbed at her and broke her necklace and pulled her silky blouse from her writhing body.

Once her hands were released, Carlyn struck at him, twisted sharply, and rolled off the other side of the wide bed, hoping to escape. Reacting quickly, Nick lunged at her with outstretched arms. His hands caught her pajama pants, pulling them from her legs. Nick pulled her back onto the bed and rolled her beneath his weight. Spent with exertion from her battle, not wanting to fight the man she loved to the depths of her heart, she lay trembling, clad in silk lace bra and panties.

"No more fighting?" Nick sneered, exalting in her capitulation.

Shaking her head no, she watched him rise to the side of the bed. His stormy eyes never left her as he removed his clothes. She flinched when he unbuckled his belt and unzipped his slacks without embarrassment, before dropping them casually to the floor. Tears shimmered in her eyes at the sight of his firmly sculpted body in snug black underpants, reminding her of their happy day sunbathing in Malibu.

"Do you always stare at your customers as they undress, or does your price include stripping them too?" he asked cruelly. The weight of his body lowering on hers pushed her deep into the soft mattress. Senses inflamed by her touch, he growled, "Tell me how you want it first, witch. Me on top . . . you on top . . . sideways . . . Come on, damn you, if you know so much, then teach me! I should get more than one for the price you charge!"

Carlyn lay passively, overpowered by his weight, the scent of his heated skin, his abrasive hair-covered chest. Her eyes were dark, her lips parted sensually.

Nick, wary of her silence and the glimmer of pain deep in her eyes, hesitated briefly before reaching for her bra. "Pretty convenient having the fastener in the front, isn't it?" He unhooked it deftly, his eyes smoldering at the sight of her flawless breasts, her pink nipples making him shake with the desire to plunder them with his mouth. But the sight of her tear-stained face and quivering lips stirred a twinge of tenderness in him that was impossible to quell.

His chest rubbed sensually against her naked breasts; his long fingers threaded through her silky hair. As he cupped her face his lips took hers with surprising gentleness, persuasively nibbling her sore mouth. Her vibrant response came unbidden, the need equal to his. His tongue teased as it probed her teeth before penetrating the sweetness of her inner mouth. His hunger, that of a man too long denied, increased as she moved against his hips.

With his steel-hard shoulders clutched in her hands Carlyn moaned deep in her throat. The touch of Nick's ardent hands sliding over her shoulders, slowly fondling her flesh, before moving to hold her breasts, stimulated a wave of awareness in the pit of her abdomen.

With trembling hands he cupped her satiny curves as his mouth sought her nipple, feeling it harden the instant his urgent mouth surrounded it. Flames blazing in his eyes, he caressed each breast alternately with the sensuous stroking of his tongue.

Moans of ecstasy escaped her lips, her nerves heightened by the volatile contact of his mouth. Her supple body curved to him, fingers sliding across his broad shoulders to his chest. In an upsurge of longing she grasped the thick dark hair over his pounding heart, her hands clenching convulsively.

Her tousled hair formed a silver aureole about her face. Tears spilled beneath her lashes as she cried out her love inwardly. Her surrender complete, she moved her hips, instinctively seeking his possession in a way as old as mankind. Her mouth parted the moment his lips returned to cling to hers in a searing kiss.

Nick slowly traced the length of her satiny body. With possessive hands he stroked her from knee to waist before exploring the soft curve of her abdomen with deliberate sensuality. Fighting hard for self-control, he stopped the downward motion of his fingers reluctantly. Her dazed expression and the passion in her slumberous eyes ignited a fire he could not extinguish. Forcing her to lay still, he groaned feverishly before crushing her mouth roughly.

His masterful skill tore Carlyn apart with unfulfilled desire. She clung to his neck, wanting to give of her entire being. Unable to keep silent any longer, she murmured against his lips, "Love me, Nick . . . please, love me."

At the sound of her words Nick pulled his lips from her face. His breathing ragged, he raised his chest, removing her clinging fingers from his nape. With narrowed eyes he stared at her body, lying golden and responsive in the dim light from the living room. Carlyn's image was imprinted on his mind and he struggled with it in his anger. The bitterness of her deception ate at his stomach like acid. But Nick could not deny his craving: he grasped her hips in his large masculine hands and lowered his face to the delicate skin of her quivering abdomen, his mouth directly over her navel.

Feeling the touch of Nick's circling tongue, Carlyn cried out wildly in unbearable need. She clasped his dark head, seeking to pull him back into her arms. "Please, Nick . . . please!"

A damp film covering his rippling shoulder muscles, defining their steel-hard strength, he abruptly stood up. He shuddered with desire, hands clenched at his sides, as he let his eyes run over her glistening body for the last time. In a deadly serious voice he commanded, "Get up, Carlyn. Get up and get the hell out! I can't take you. I thought I could, but even with your languorous body and passion-darkened eyes begging I can't blot out the image of your life-style. I'm unable to equate the innocence I feel when I kiss you with your admitted . . . profession. May God forgive you, Carlyn," he sighed regretfully, "because I sure as hell can't. Now get up, dammit! Get the hell out of my life!"

His eyes never sought her as he dressed with his back to her, uncaring that she lay curled on her side, whimpering softly, heartbroken and defenseless.

Unmoved by her tears, he commanded, "I said get out! Get your damn clothes on and get out now." His eyes were hard, his expression icy as he repeated, "I don't want to see you, hear you, or feel you again." Pivoting on his heels, he stormed out of the room.

Limp with fatigue from her upheaval with Nick, Carlyn dressed. Purse in hand, she fled his room, her body trembling so bad, she could hardly move. As she entered her suite she was grasped by Tim, his face white with panic at her temporary disappearance.

"My God, what happened to you? We've been frantic," Tim exclaimed, nodding toward George, who sat observing them silently. "We knew you weren't with Benny or his men because we just left them. Ralph is checking on

Marie's whereabouts now. Who was the man in the bar you talked with?" Voice rising, he gasped, "For God's sake, tell me!"

"Leave her be, Carlson," George warned him, reading the distress on Carlyn's face.

She turned her back when Tim released his hold so that they would not see the tears still visible on her colorless face. Head lowered dejectedly, she pleaded, "Give me a few minutes to gather myself together please. I—I want to shower and change, then I'll explain."

"Okay. That will give George time to find Ralph and let him know you're safe," Tim said, motioning the sergeant to leave.

In her room Carlyn tore her clothes off, throwing them in the wastebasket. The sharp spray of the shower stung her bruised body like splinters. Scrubbing over and over, she let the water wash the feel of Benny's lustful touch and Nick's punishing caresses down the drain. Dressed in a full-length navy-blue velour robe buttoned to the throat, she entered the living room. Her hair was brushed smoothly, her face free of makeup, and she was fragrant with her own flowery perfume—her beauty was pure and touching. She felt her true self again after turbulent days and a lifetime's education.

Tim's eyes filled with compassion as he sat beside her on the couch. "We have to know about it, honey, so start at the beginning."

Carlyn knew she could never tell anyone the depth of her feelings for Nick, least of all her co-workers. She skimmed over the intimate details, telling Tim he was a man she had met and dated a few weeks previously. She admitted they had been emotionally involved and had parted over a lack of communication. "You don't need to worry," she reassured him. "I'll continue with the assignment. He thinks I'm a . . . prostitute and will never attempt to contact me again. He's too proud," she added sadly.

"Go lie down while I check with the front desk and see how long this Nick is staying. I'll explain to Ralph and George about it."

Carlyn sighed with relief at hearing the door close behind Tim. The additional privacy was welcome. She went to her room and forcing her body to relax, lay on the soft mattress, her mind heavy with despair over her accidental meeting with Nick and the disastrous events that followed. Aroused from her stupor by a gentle knock, she opened the door a slight crack.

Tim held an envelope to her. "I thought you might be waiting to hear. The clerk said Nick checked out suddenly, leaving this at the desk for you. Back to bed, honey, and sweet dreams." His sharp eyes noticed the poignant look and fresh tears on her cheeks.

She closed the door before Tim could inquire about her, and sat on the edge of the bed hesitating before opening the envelope, dreading its contents. She expected a harshly worded note; she did not expect what stared at her from her palm—the face of President Cleveland mocking her from the front of two crisp new one-thousand-dollar bills.

She was devastated. She knew that this was Nick's way of telling her his love had ended in one explosive encounter. *It's over,* she cried. *There's nothing I can do now.* She threw the money into her purse, removed her robe, and turned out the light. Emotionally spent, she tossed restlessly. Her hours awake were more of a nightmare than any dream could be.

CHAPTER ELEVEN

Carlyn listened intently as their plans were adjusted to meet Benny's early departure. George and Ralph left the suite, intent on the crucial talk with Marie. The moment she agreed to testify, the captain's backup team, briefed and waiting, would make the arrest. Benny nor Marie would be aware of Tim or Carlyn's part in the drama. Within hours Carlyn knew she should be in her home, enjoying a few days rest before reporting back to regular duty.

Tim nervously paced the floor, repeatedly glancing at his watch, impatient for the morning to pass. A feeling of unease grew into deep concern as it neared noon and he hadn't heard from his men. Apprehensive, he scrutinized Carlyn as she stood at the window. "What time did you tell Benny you'd go to his room?" he asked grimly.

Glancing over her shoulder, nerves tense, "Noon," she replied.

Irritation at not hearing from his men and knowing all he could do was wait caused him to exclaim angrily, "It's nearly that now." Rubbing the back of his neck, he sighed glumly.

Carlyn's voice was firm and confident as she turned to face him. "Let me go to Benny's room as planned so my cover won't be endangered. If I don't arrive on time, you know he'll get suspicious and look for me."

"Too risky," Tim answered seriously. "My gut tells me that something's about to erupt. I can't shake the feeling of impending disaster." They heard a knock and he ran, sighing with relief, to the door.

"Where have you two been?" he demanded as George and Ralph slipped into the room. "What's up? Did she agree to testify?"

Wiping beads of nervous sweat from his brow, George explained, "We had one hell of a time getting her alone to interrogate. She's finally convinced we'll give her protection from Benny and his men but she only agreed to divulge information on his activities if we let her collect her furs and jewelry. She admitted he'd told her to leave."

"Why couldn't she get her stuff after Valouse's arrest?" Tim argued, displeased she wasn't isolated from further contact with him.

"She wouldn't have it, Lieutenant. She was adamant that she'd go into protective custody wearing her mink coat and carrying all her jewelry," Ralph added, also vexed by her stubbornness.

"How'd she take it?" Tim questioned curiously.

"Surprisingly calm."

"Carlyn promised to meet Benny at noon and wants to go down until the captain's men arrive. What do you two think? Should we risk it?" Tim asked gravely, looking at his partners apprehensively.

"You know I'm right, Tim. It's late and he's impatient." Carlyn interrupted, reminding them that she wouldn't be in Benny's room long.

"Okay, but it's against my better judgment. Keep cool, play dumb, and slip out of the room the minute our men arrive. His three goons will be picked up in the bar where they're waiting to give you and Valouse privacy for your party. If things go smoothly, the hotel guests won't know what happened until they read the newspaper."

Admiring Carlyn's determination, Tim squeezed her arm. "George and Ralph will wait outside Benny's room in case you need them, while I meet the captain's team in the lobby. It appears now as if the L.A.P.D.'s going to get credit for one hell of a bust." Tim cupped her chin. "Get going and good luck." Watching thoughtfully as she left the room, he wished the feeling of unease would leave. George and Ralph followed behind her to take their positions. "Maybe I'm getting an ulcer," he grumbled to the empty room.

Benny opened the door to his suite, overcome by her beauty as she stood there, suitcase in hand. His eyes traveled intimately over her gray crepe-de-chine blouse and short skirt. Carlyn shuddered at the sight of him clad in a maroon satin dressing gown, snug across his stocky body. She was thankful her nightmare would soon end.

As she walked into the center of the large suite, his hooded eyes lingered on her curves outlined by the soft material. "It'll be a few minutes before my ex-broad vacates the bedroom. She's in there gathering her mink coat and jewelry," Benny said, reaching out to take the suitcase from Carlyn and set it down. "You'll be the most envied blonde in New York when I get through dressing you, baby," he bragged. "A ring on each finger and soft fur from head to toe."

"Sounds great, Benny," Carlyn lied, waiting as he moved toward her.

Placing his powerful arms around her back, he drew her close, his heavy paunch touching her flat stomach. A forced smile tugged at her lips as his head bent to place his mouth over hers.

As she turned sideways to avoid his mouth, Carlyn

noticed the bedroom door open. Marie walked out, her lustrous mink draped over one arm, completely covering her hand. Twisting in Benny's hold, Carlyn stood facing his ex-mistress, her expression calm.

"Get a move on, Marie," he told her curtly. "You're taking up time better spent in the bedroom." To emphasize his meaning he spread his hand over Carlyn's hip and placed a long kiss on the side of her neck. His eyes filled with contempt as he deliberately taunted Marie.

Tension in the room mounted. Perspiration beaded Carlyn's brow as she felt her body react to the element of impending disaster. Senses alerted to a sudden shift of emotions, sensitive to moods, she knew Marie's hostilities were reaching the point of hysteria.

Standing in front of Benny, who obtusely continued to aggravate the situation by fondling Carlyn's hip and waist, she watched Marie's eyes, waiting for a clue to her next move. Hoping her calmness would have a soothing effect she stood motionless, mind thinking rapidly.

"Get moving, you stupid bitch!" Benny sneered, his lust for Carlyn making him careless.

Marie's face whitened, her eyes seethed with fury, and she raged at him. "You think you know so much, you filthy bastard? Did you know your days of power are over? Your blonde happens to be a policewoman with the L.A.P.D., and you fell like an overripe plum into their trap!"

Carlyn sensed the danger before actually seeing the barrel end of a small thirty-eight caliber pistol held securely in Marie's trembling hand.

Without thought for her own safety, Carlyn pushed her hip into Benny, hoping to knock him out of the line of fire before diving for the gun in Marie's clasp.

Benny, bellowing like a maddened bull and off balance, managed to take his heavy fist and slam it into the side of Carlyn's head before lunging at his ex-mistress. He was enraged at being duped; his one desire was to destroy—Marie or Carlyn—it didn't matter.

Fearing for her life, Marie fired. The first shot entered Carlyn's left side as she staggered from the blow to her head. She was unconscious before she hit the floor, abdomen bleeding profusely. The second shot struck Benny in the chest. He collapsed heavily, blood spreading slowly over the front of his robe, the color matching the satin of his gown.

Simultaneous with the sound of gunfire the door was kicked open and the room immediately filled with plainclothes police.

Tim's darting eyes focused on the figure of Carlyn lying in a crumpled heap. He yelled to George to call an ambulance and ran to her side to check for life, giving a silent prayer when he felt a shallow pulsebeat. She lay unconscious, bleeding profusely from her abdomen. Applying pressure to stop the bleeding, he looked with leaden eyes at Ralph.

Squatting on his heels next to him, Ralph told him, "Valouse is dead." His eyes filled with remorse as he stared at Carlyn's body. "How's Carlyn?"

"If the ambulance ever gets here we'll find out. What the hell's keeping them?" Tim cried out in desperation. "She's bleeding so bad, I can't stop it with my hand. I don't think I could stand it if she died." As Tim cradled her head Ralph and George stood by, feeling helpless at their inability to do more. She remained quiet, breathing shallowly, her face drained of all color.

Marie stood in the corner, eyes glazed, body shaking, pistol at her feet. "I didn't mean to hurt her, only him," she repeated over and over. "She pushed him, or I wouldn't have hit her."

Hearing the sound of the ambulance crew rushing down the hall, the officers motioned them to take care of Carlyn. "Leave him for the coroner," the lieutenant ordered.

Tim, face shocked, eyes filled with pain, said huskily to his partners, "Thank God he's dead. I'd have killed him myself if Carlyn doesn't make it." As the ambulance crew placed her on a stretcher, he cried out in a hoarse voice, "Look at her, she's so damned innocent, I could cry at the injustice of it all." He commanded his men tersely to take care of all the notifications.

The slight jarring of the stretcher caused Carlyn to regain consciousness for a brief moment. Her eyes focused on Tim: she whispered, her voice barely audible in the busy room, "Sorry, Tim, guess I blew it for you and the captain."

"Don't talk, honey," he pleaded, staring at her glazing violet eyes. "You did great. You're going to be fine, perfectly fine."

Unaware of Tim cursing at the seriousness of her injury, she slipped into oblivion. The siren blared as the ambulance sped to the hospital emergency entrance. She was whisked off to the operating room, where a team of surgeons, having been alerted, were waiting. Carlyn remained unconscious as she was wheeled from surgery to intensive care.

Press and television crews crowded the corridors, anxious to take pictures and get details of the newsworthy shooting. Captain Stinson arrived to find Tim pacing the waiting room while George and Ralph sipped their third cup of bitter coffee. His arrival coincided with that of Dr. Hargrove who stepped from the elevator still clad in his green surgical gown. Holding his hand up, he assured them, "Relax, she'll be fine. The bullet passed through her left side with no serious internal damage. She's a very lucky young woman. An inch more to the right and she'd have been in grave danger." After explaining in detail about her surgery and future recuperation, he told them they could take a quick look to reassure themselves that she was all right.

The men looked solemnly at her still form, seemingly dwarfed by the large equipment and monitors at her bedside. Her pale face was a startling background for her black lashes. Her silvery hair, still vibrant with life, glimmered in disarray around her face.

Each of the men was overcome by a feeling of helplessness and, in his own way, said a silent prayer for her. They brushed rudely past the newsmen on their way out, telling them to go to Parker Center for a complete statement later that evening. Riding with the captain to headquarters, Tim inhaled deeply on a cigarette before relating the sequence of events. His hands shaking uncontrollably, he laughed bitterly, "Look at me, I've been in shoot-outs before and never flinched, but seeing Carlyn has given me the shakes." After listening attentively, the captain explained to him that Marie had been booked for the murder of Benny and the attempted murder of Carlyn. The three bodyguards were being interrogated while run for warrants.

Later, seated in his office, his eyes pinning his men, Captain Stinson spoke. "What went wrong?"

Tim, seated in front of the desk, leaned his forehead in his hands, and said in a muffled voice, "I don't know. Maybe nothing. Maybe everything. I had a feeling of doom when we had to rush our plans."

Leaning against the wall, the fringe of red hair vivid against his pale forehead, George exclaimed harshly, "I'm to blame, Captain. I was so eager to get his mistress to testify, I agreed to her demand to get her things. God, I never dreamed the bitch had a gun!"

"Don't blame yourself. I was in charge, and it was my decision to let her go to Benny's room alone," Tim disputed him, glaring at his partner. "The only good thing that happened was his death."

Ralph agreed vehemently but reminded them, "There's more like him."

Suddenly Tim remembered and blurted out, "Man, I must be in shock. Did anyone think to notify her father?"

Captain Stinson nodded. "He took it calmly, considering. He's due in on a nine o'clock flight tonight."

"Doesn't she have a brother in Santa Monica also?" Tim inquired.

The captain nodded. "They should be at the hospital now. Doug Thomas felt it would be less of a shock if he phoned his son, as they all thought she was out of town—"

His explanation was interrupted by a ring of the phone. The captain talked briefly, then notified his men. "That was downtown. The reporters have settled in. This will be front-page news. They've seen her picture and know how beautiful she is."

"Marie said Carlyn tried to push Valouse out of the way. Can you imagine anyone trying to save that bastard's life?" Tim groaned.

"This is what the general public rarely realizes," the captain reminded them. "Our motto is 'To protect and to serve'—there isn't a police officer who would hesitate to do just that."

Tim agreed, "Like Carlyn. She hated every minute of this assignment after making contact with Valouse, yet she never faltered. I could have killed him when he dared to touch her."

Dismissing his men abruptly, Captain Stinson began filling out reports, an endless task on any assignment. He glanced at his watch after finishing late that afternoon. Blunt fingers rubbing the tension from his brow, he decided to have dinner, then pick up his old friend at the airport.

Carlyn lay unaware of the events taking place around her or of the many people concerned about her safety. Lieutenant Carlson and the others had already called to find out about her condition, and the nursing staff had

171

been alerted to monitor her constantly. Her vital signs were holding stable.

Smoking his fifth cigarette, Captain Stinson watched the 727 jet taxi to a smooth stop. As the passengers departed he spotted Doug's worried face towering over the heads of the people before him. A tall, well-built man, he was obviously showing impatience at the slowness of those ahead.

"How is she, Jack?" he asked anxiously, shaking the captain's hand automatically.

"Fine, Doug, she'll be just fine," he assured him.

"I think I aged ten years hearing your news," Doug remarked, following him to the police car. He flung his suitcase into the backseat and got in. "I was lucky to make such good connections, but not knowing if my daughter was alive or not was unbearable."

"Did you get in touch with your son?" the captain inquired as he eased the blue Ford onto the busy northbound 405 freeway.

"Yes. They'll be at the hospital. What a family reunion this is." Looking over the familiar dull interior of the police car, he grimaced. "God, it's been three years since I retired, but sitting in a city car makes it seem like yesterday. Even smells the same—stale cigarette smoke. Okay, Jack, spill it. I want to know all the details, every single damn thing that happened to my baby girl."

By the time the entire chain of events leading to the shooting had been related, they arrived at the hospital. "Carlyn's on the third floor in intensive care. I'll park and come on up."

Doug's long strides took him quickly to the elevator. As the third-floor doors parted, the antiseptic smell struck him, reminding him unnecessarily that his beloved daughter lay behind one of the impersonal doors on each side of the wide corridor. Spotting his son and daughter-in-law,

172

he rushed to them. Father and son grasped each other in welcome.

"She's doing fine, Dad. Sleeping under heavy sedation. The nurse says she won't remember a thing that happened today."

Hugging his petite daughter-in-law, he observed her tears. Bob guided him to Carlyn's door, and Doug entered when the nurse motioned.

Standing by the bed, he received his worst shock at the pitiful sight of her still form and stark white face. Dark lashes forming crescents above her drawn cheeks, she looked vulnerable and helpless. But he felt reassured by the steady rise and fall of her breasts. He whispered to the nurse, "How's my daughter? She'll recover, won't she?"

Admiring the honesty and strength of the striking-looking man, the nurse smiled, consoling him instantly with her confident manner. "Yes, Mr. Thomas, she'll be just fine."

Throughout the long night father and son waited in the small visitors room for Carlyn to awaken. Marianne had driven home to care for the children and arrange for a baby-sitter for the next day.

As the sun rose, the dawn-tinted sky changing from rose to hazy gold, Carlyn began to stir restlessly in the hospital bed. Still sedated, she was unaware of her pitiful whimpering as she cried for Nick over and over in a soft, pleading voice.

But Doug heard his daughter's cries and turned to Bob, questioning who Nick was. Bob explained the little he knew about Carlyn's relationship with the man she had known for five days in Malibu.

"She fell pretty hard for the guy, who at first appeared to feel the same about her but then ditched her."

"My God!" Doug exclaimed as they walked to the waiting room. "The poor baby. As far as I know, he's her first real love interest too." He dropped some coins into the vending machine and steadied the cup as the coffee poured into it. After handing it to his son, he repeated the procedure and sat down. "Who is he, Bob? Do you know anything at all about him?"

"Only what Marianne told me," Bob replied, leaning his elbows on his knees, the untouched cup of coffee dangling in his hands. "We never met him, of course, but Carlyn told Marianne that he's an admitted womanizer, a millionaire, owns restaurants, and lives in San Francisco, I believe—although they met in Malibu."

"Damn the man! How could anybody walk away from my daughter?"

"Be fair, Dad. We know how lovely Carlyn is, but maybe this Nick didn't take the time or care enough to find out."

Doug nodded his head in agreement, his honesty forcing him to admit his son was probably right. His thoughts were interrupted by Carlyn's nurse, Miss Sanderson, who touched his shoulder compassionately. "Mr. Thomas, you're wanted on the phone. A Captain Stinson calling."

At his friend's inquiry Doug explained, "She's fine as far as the surgery goes, but she seems restless and depressed. Keeps calling for some guy named Nick. As soon as we've talked with the doctor, we're going to go home, catch a couple hours sleep, and clean up." After talking briefly, they said their good-byes. Turning to his son, he told him, "We better get today's paper. Jack said Carlyn made headlines and they wrote a flattering report. She'll want to see them when she's well. Something to save for her future as a reminder of her close call." They looked up to see the doctor approach.

Dr. Hargrove, immaculately groomed in a tailored three-piece suit, his gray hair and goatee neatly trimmed, introduced himself and reassured the men that Carlyn would be fine, other than her being distressed about a man named Nick. His nurses had noted that she kept calling for him throughout the night.

They left after the doctor's visit but returned early that evening. Refreshed after the rest and change of clothing, they were greeted by Jack and Tim. After everyone had been introduced, Doug informed them of the doctor's news.

Tim explained to Doug about Carlyn meeting a man named Nick during her undercover work as a prostitute. "They apparently had a traumatic confrontation in his suite afterward. She was very distressed after the meeting. Nick checked out of the hotel immediately afterward but left Carlyn a note at the hotel desk. She never mentioned his name after that. I don't know if that's making her fret, but she was on the point of collapse after she saw him." His obvious concern for Carlyn showed in his anxiety and desire to help.

"Thanks for the information, Tim. I think I understand the situation a little more clearly now. I hope you'll excuse me, please, I want to go see my daughter." He shook hands with the two men, then proceeded to Carlyn's room.

CHAPTER TWELVE

Carlyn woke slowly. Her first conscious thought was the sharp burning pain in her left side and a dull, throbbing headache. The seemingly impenetrable mist cleared as she remembered each event in total recall. Thankful to be alive, she lay still, letting her shadowed eyes roam the stark white ceiling, the suspended bottles of fluid, and sophisticated emergency equipment.

The ache in her head increased painfully as she turned, and she wished for the painless oblivion of deep sleep. Tentatively moving her limbs, she moaned, attracting the nurse's attention.

"How are you feeling, Miss Thomas?"

"Kind of groggy." Her voice was soft, still weak from shock.

"Are you in pain, dear?" Nurse Sanderson questioned as she took her pulse. "You've been unconscious for quite a while now."

"Quite a bit, but I'm happy just to be alive," she whispered seriously. "Everything happened so fast. Does— does my father know?"

"Yes, he was here all night long and should be returning

176

soon. You're quite the celebrity. You've been on television, headlined in the newspapers, and the hospital's been deluged with calls from people concerned about you. Your flowers could stock a nursery."

"Has anyone else been to see me?" Carlyn asked wistfully.

"Like who, dear?" she asked kindly. "Your brother and sister-in-law, plus scores of police, but no other specific names I know of." She didn't want to mention his name, felt it better that Carlyn brought it up herself, in case it conjured painful memories.

Disappointed, Carlyn sighed wearily, her bruised eyes shimmering with unshed tears. Suddenly weak from talking, she lay quiet, knowing she was foolish to expect Nick to come to her. Her heart ached with desire to see his eyes looking at her with love shining in their depths.

Exhausted, she rested. Her tightly closed eyelids could not dam the tears as they trickled down her smooth cheeks. She didn't hear the quiet sound of her father's footsteps as he entered the room, didn't see the pain in his eyes as he stared at her forlorn face, but was aware instantly of the comfort she felt as he touched her hand.

Her eyes opened the moment she felt his callous palm. She was overcome with emotion, crying at the sight of her father's face, his loving glance a balm to her weakened body and dejected mind. "Oh, Daddy, I'm so happy you're here. I need you so badly," she murmured, her lips trembling with despondency.

Her poignant voice tearing at his heart, he bent over his daughter and kissed her tenderly on the cheek, unashamedly weeping in joy to have her safe. She was infinitely dear to him, her mother's image.

"Don't cry, Daddy. I'm fine now that you're here," she said, weeping, holding tightly to his large hands with tightly clenched fingers.

"If your father wasn't gray haired already, daughter of

mine, this would have done it. It will take time to sink in that you are actually safe. I haven't been so shocked since your mother died."

As she smiled weakly her violet eyes glimmered with love. "I'll be fine, Daddy. We Thomases are made of pretty sturdy stock." With a puzzled expression she asked, "How did his mistress know I was a police officer? No one but George and Ralph talked to her from the department."

Relieved to be conversing with her, he was aware from the depth of despair in her pain-filled eyes that his visit was not bringing total succor. "I don't know, love, but I'll find out from Jack."

Doug straightened as the nurse interrupted. "Good evening, Mr. Thomas. I'm sorry but you'll have to leave. Your son and his wife can say hello briefly, but we have to give your daughter medication." Smiling sympathetically, she continued, "Tomorrow she'll be moved to a private room. Eleven is a good time."

Broad shoulders dwarfing Carlyn's figure, he placed a kiss on each cheek and wiped the tears away tenderly with his palm. Squeezing her hand, he held it to him, love flowing between them. He left her when Nurse Sanderson entered with Bob and Marianne. Seeing Carlyn for the first time since her injury, they had an emotional reunion in the sterile hospital room.

As the nurse followed Doug into the hall she asked to speak to him privately, then led him to an empty office. Admiring her tiny shapely figure, he waited calmly for her to speak.

He listened attentively to her soft voice, which soothed his tension. "Your daughter appears to be suffering from not seeing a man named Nick, and the distress will not aid in her recuperation. Do you suppose you could find him? She cried his name pitifully throughout the night."

"I don't know the man, but if I find him, he'll visit her,"

he told her grimly. "Thank you for your interest, Nurse Sanderson."

Impressed by his quiet manner and family devotion, she smiled warmly at him, then went back to duty.

Deliberating, Doug walked into the waiting room. When he saw Captain Stinson, he said, "Glad you're still here, Jack. I've got a favor to ask. Carlyn keeps calling for a stranger and I wondered if one of your men could find out where I can get in touch with him." He looked with brooding eyes at his friend. "I refuse to allow my daughter's recovery to be hindered by any man. If she wants Nick, by God, she'll have him. They can straighten out their problems after she's well."

Pleased to be able to help, Jack was given what information Doug knew, agreeing to let him know as soon as possible what he found.

"Oh, another thing, Jack. Carlyn can't understand how Valouse's mistress knew she was a police officer."

Bob and Marianne listened unbelievingly as he explained what transpired. "It was an undercover officer's nightmare. The bellboy who carried in their luggage that first day recognized her. He had watched television coverage of Carlyn's graduating class at the Police Academy almost four years earlier. The kid has a gift for remembering faces and he was so impressed that a girl as beautiful as Carlyn would want to work as a policewoman that her image remained imprinted on his mind. When he helped Marie with her baggage, he mentioned the story to her just to make conversation. It nearly cost your daughter her life."

"My God, how little we realize what danger an unthinking word to the wrong person can cause," Doug sighed in astonishment.

"For what it's worth, we accomplished far more than we had hoped. We have several indictments pending now. Carlyn's courage and dedication were very heroic indeed." Wishing the three a good-night, he left at the same time, parting in the lobby.

Early the next morning Carlyn's father received a phone call from Jack telling him they had contacted the owner of the house at Malibu where Nick stayed. "He's Dr. Brett Masters, a prominent area psychiatrist. I talked with him a minute ago. He agreed to meet you at his office at ten but would tell me nothing about Nick."

Promptly at ten o'clock Doug entered Dr. Masters's office, curious about his encounter. Impressed by the stranger's direct look and intelligent face, he felt confident the doctor would help him ease Carlyn's distress.

Beginning without preamble, Dr. Masters told him bluntly, "Captain Stinson explained the situation and I agreed to meet you because of my sympathy for your daughter. I understand you are attempting to locate Nick Sandini, who was a recent guest at my home in Malibu?" Leaning back in his chair, he watched Doug intently.

"Correct, although I didn't know his last name. My daughter is deeply distressed at this womanizer's treatment of her," Doug retorted grimly.

Dr. Masters held up his hand to stop the verbal attack on his friend. "You are misinformed, Mr. Thomas. Nick is a trusted friend and not a womanizer in the true sense of the word. I will not allow you to malign him without hearing the facts. I agree Nick leads an active social life, but he is also a serious, hardworking man who holds the responsibility of a large chain of restaurants and hundreds of employees in his hands—and most capably too. He is wealthy, in the prime of life, handsome, and single. Each of these things would make him popular with women; combined, they make him irresistible to many. To my knowledge he has never misled any woman about his intentions. The world is full of sophisticates, Mr. Thomas. Would you deny Nick the company of consenting women

180

well aware there can be no permanence to their relationship? Would you deny him a social life?"

"No, of course not," Doug admitted honestly. "My only concern is that my daughter apparently believed his attentions were serious, and they weren't. Carlyn hasn't spoken to me about Nick. I am going on hearsay from my son. She is heartbroken over this man, and I feel in all human decency he should be persuaded to visit her."

"Tell me about your daughter, Mr. Thomas." Dr. Masters listened attentively; his interest in human behavior was insatiable.

Eased by the doctor's calm concern, Doug told him briefly about Carlyn's life: her apparent disinterest in the numerous young men who sought her attentions since early maturity; her aptness as a brilliant student, avid reader, excellent cook and homemaker; and her strong desire to be a policewoman. "One I discouraged at each opportunity," he added grimly. "Her emotional involvement was almost nil before she met Nick. Can you understand what a shock it was to me to hear her pleading fervently for your friend? She confessed to my daughter-in-law that she loves Nick more than anything in the world. I guarantee you she has never felt the least concern for another man."

"It appears there has been a terrible misunderstanding between them, and puts an entirely different view on the matter." His glance thoughtful, his voice concerned, he explained, "The night Carlyn was wounded, Nick awakened me at two in the morning. I noticed immediately he was distressed, seriously disturbed, in fact. Since I had last seen him, he had lost weight and paced nervously—quite unlike his normal manner. After much questioning he admitted he had met a girl in Malibu, fallen in love immediately, and believed her to be innocent. Most important to him she seemed to return his love, which was serious from their first meeting.

"Nick had to leave for New York suddenly and asked Carlyn to marry him. She was to give him her answer when he returned. Imagine his shock on finding she had left without even a note of explanation. Their only problem had been Carlyn's evasiveness about her work. He was frantic when he couldn't find her. He had no address or phone number, but he spared no expense to locate her. He refused to leave the L.A. area despite his urgent business commitments."

"My God, I had no idea," Doug said sympathetically.

"That isn't the worst. Nick was in agony telling me. He's a proud man and found it impossible that he had misjudged your daughter so badly. Angered beyond reason when he spotted her working as a call girl, he demanded the favors he thought she was selling. But he felt ashamed and bitter and left prior to the consummation. His final gesture was to send Carlyn two thousand dollars payment. Your daughter may be unhappy, but Nick is a broken man. He left early the next morning for northern California, hoping to erase the shock of her life-style from his mind, her love from his heart."

"Where can I reach him?" Doug asked as the doctor stood.

"He has no telephone or television and receives no newspapers. He won't have any idea what has happened, I'm sure. I'll give you his address. How you contact him will be your choice."

Anxious to make arrangements to leave Los Angeles, Doug shook his hand and thanked him for his help. Dr. Masters's astounding news had dismayed him and he knew it imperative he act quickly and wisely for the welfare of his daughter and the man she loved.

Alone in a private room, Carlyn lay passive, her hands nervously plucking at the sheet as she remembered her traumatic meeting with Nick. His sudden change in physical appearance, the weight loss, and anger remained

182

locked in her mind. He hadn't even mentioned her note. Tormented with memories of his harsh words and brutal rejection, she closed her eyes, unaware that the door opened.

Entering the room, Doug noticed her teary cheeks. Her sorrow tore at his heart and made him even more impatient to find Nick. With forced cheerfulness he kissed her face, her startled eyes opening in a brilliant flash of violet. "Good morning, sweet daughter of mine. Are you in a lot of pain today?" Pulling a chair forward, he sat facing her, his broad palm dwarfing her slender hand.

"No, Daddy. I'm fine really. These are just silly girl tears," she stated slowly, attempting to explain the reason for crying.

"I'm glad you're in a private room. It means you're healing without complications. I need to know you will be okay before I leave you. I want to fly home for a couple days to get things in order. Then I can stay here until you're out of the hospital and able to care for yourself again. It's a wonder I turned off the coffeepot, I left in such a hurry." He continued to hold her hand affectionately, his touch assuring her that the horrors of the past few days would gradually recede.

"Hurry back, Daddy," she cried pathetically. "I—I need you so much now." Clinging to his fingers, she told him she had asked Nurse Sanderson to see that she didn't have visitors. "Do you understand how I feel, Daddy? I don't feel up to any more questions yet. Will you notify the captain for me? I—I want to be alone until I'm home."

"Excellent idea, love. Everyone will appreciate your reasons. Nurse Sanderson seems competent and I'm sure she'll see you're not bothered."

Carlyn's silver hair formed a crown around her face as she teased impudently, "She asked me about you, Daddy, in case you're interested. She has been wonderful to me.

Even thinks you are the most handsome man she has ever met."

"Don't go making plans for me, minx!" he laughed back.

Undaunted, she continued, "She's been a widow for four years. Her husband had been injured in the Air Force and confined to a wheelchair for several years. Linda hasn't had an easy life, Daddy."

"Has any of us?" he asked thoughtfully, thinking of his wife's death and Carlyn's problems. "I'm a confirmed widower, remember? Besides, who would want to take on a man my age who lives in the country and devotes all his spare time to fishing and gardening?"

"I have a feeling Linda would think that was ideal."

"Hush now, love. I have to leave."

As he stepped into the hall he observed Nurse Sanderson checking records at the nurses station. "Could I ask a favor of you?" Remembering his daughter's words, he noticed the golden glints in her soft brown eyes, how immaculate her white uniform was, the shiny curls that escaped under her white cap. "I have to leave for a day or two and would like you to see that Carlyn doesn't have any visitors."

"I've already taken care of it, Mr. Thomas," she told him.

"Please call me Doug, and if I may, I would like to take you to dinner when I return, Linda. I'm staying with my son and his family and think it best if I give them some privacy. I would be delighted to have your company when you're not working."

"Sounds wonderful, Doug." She smiled, eyes sparkling with pleasure.

"I told Carlyn I have to return home but actually I'm hoping to get in touch with Nick." In a hurry Doug said good-bye and left.

Within two hours he had returned to his son's home,

packed, taken a taxi to the airport, and was airborne. The drone of the sleek 727 pounded through his mind, its powerful jet engines taking him quickly north.

He watched with casual interest as the plane banked to circuit the azure-blue bay of San Francisco. Towering high-rise buildings, the undulating sea of rooftops covering rolling hills, the never-ending traffic, barely registered as they circled to land. The famed Golden Gate and Oakland Bay bridges joined the cosmopolitan city with areas north, their spans stretching gracefully across the water.

The plane bumped twice before coming to an abrupt halt on the concrete runway. Impatient to be on his way, he was uncaring of the rough landing. He rented a car and was soon traveling north on Highway One toward the town of Fort Bragg near Nick's home.

CHAPTER THIRTEEN

Nick sat on his redwood deck, tired and low in spirits, long legs stretched before him. The distant view had never before failed to inspire him with a feeling of faith and peace, yet he took no notice of the stately redwoods and surging Pacific Ocean.

Twinging pain in his aching shoulders prompted him to recall all the firewood he had split. Enough to last him at least three years, he grimaced. Disgusted over his inability to sleep, despite the back-breaking physical exertion of the previous days, he knew the cause: It was the constant thought of Carlyn.

Her image refused to leave his mind no matter how he cursed himself for being so foolish. Clasping his aching forehead in his palms, he leaned forward, the muscles on his broad back rippling visibly beneath the sweat-stained shirt that clung to his body. He groaned with anxiety, knowing he still loved her and would always love her.

Making a spur-of-the-moment decision, he went to his bedroom. He threw his soiled clothes to the floor, let the tingling shower massage his body, then dressed, anxious to return to San Francisco and bury himself in his neglected restaurant business. For the first time in his life work had been unimportant to his happiness.

The Porsche responded instantly to his touch as he accelerated down the graveled drive to the main highway. Turning south, he started the long winding drive down the northern California coast. A glance at his watch told him he'd reach home shortly after dusk, enabling him to resume work the following day.

The silver sports car hugging the turns of the narrow mountainous highway, he arrived without mishap. His attention had never wavered from the road, uncaring of the beauty of the coastline. Greeted by his servants as he entered his luxurious main residence, he nodded briefly before going to his suite, where he spent long hours alone and brooding, trying to adjust to life without Carlyn.

A raging headache attested to his night of drinking when he entered his study the next morning. Freshly showered, he looked a totally confident businessman as he thumbed casually through his accumulated mail. Rubbing his chin, he pondered an invitation, the breadth of his shoulders outlined in the thin silk of his cerulean-blue shirt and suit vest. Navy-blue slacks, excellently tailored to his narrow hips, clung as he lay the mail on his desk. Gathering up several out of town newspapers, he prepared to drop them into the wastebasket.

As it fell from his hand he bent to pick up the bottom paper and looked straight into the face of Carlyn, pictured on the front page. His face ashen, he read the bold headline print, POLICEWOMAN SHOT. He scanned the story, hands shaking, blood flowing through his veins, as he read she was alive and recovering in a Hollywood hospital.

Nick rang for his servant. Within minutes his suitcase was packed, flight booked, main office contacted and he was driving to the airport.

Filled with remorse over his previous treatment of Carlyn, he wondered how he could have ever doubted her innocence. Throughout the fifty-five-minute flight to Los Angeles and twenty-mile drive to the hospital he was unable to understand her evasiveness about her work. He shuddered thinking of her close call with death.

As Nick cursed the heavy freeway traffic, Carlyn was talking with Linda. "You can't imagine how much better I feel after a bath and putting on a soft nightgown. I much prefer my own lingerie to that hospital gown," she chortled, walking cautiously to her bed in a deep plum satin gown with ivory lace trim.

"You look lovely, dear. The color highlights your eyes. You must remember to keep your bed jacket on during the day or all our young interns will be in here instead of attending to their rounds." After Linda squared the corners of the fresh-made bed and plumped the pillow, she turned to Carlyn and smiled warmly. "Ready for a rest now?"

Agreeing without hesitation, Carlyn lay back, disgusted with herself for feeling so weak her first day on her feet. As she closed her eyes she listened to Linda's soothing voice explaining she would leave her alone until lunch.

Dozing in the lightly shadowed room, Carlyn began to dream of Nick, distressing thoughts causing her to whimper his name. The loneliness and despair over Nick's loss racked her body with sobs, and tears trickled steadily down her smooth cheeks.

Nick strode purposefully down the hall, stopping at the nurses station to inquire the number of Carlyn's room.

"It's three-oh-five, sir, but there's no visitors allowed," the nurse's aide told him politely.

Unheedingly Nick abruptly walked toward the room, the aide calling out behind him. He entered unhesitantly, unaware that the startled aide had rushed to her supervisor for assistance.

Her poignant voice crying his name, the shock of her slim body in the dim hospital room, was more than he could bear. He touched her tenderly, his breath fanning her face as he whispered huskily, "It's Nick, sweetheart . . . Oh, God, please don't cry, darling. I love you and I can't stand to hear you suffer." His chest heaving with the depth of his feelings, he pleaded, "Please, my love . . . no more tears."

The sound of his emotion-filled voice invaded the depths of her sleep. Her eyes fluttered open and saw a clouded, but familiar, image bending before her. "Nick!" she cried, feeling as though she were dreaming. Tears shimmered in her eyes as she reached out for him, desperate to feel his steel-hard shoulders and know he was really there. "Oh, Nick, it's really you," she cried incredulously at the miracle of his appearance.

Head bowed in a prayer of thanks for her safety, he cupped her face reverently with trembling palms. Her glance revealed a look of such love and caring, he thought his heart would stop with happiness. Fingers threading through the silken hair that tumbled over her pillow, he lowered his head slowly, "I always loved you, darling. Never doubt that—" His words of adoration were cut quickly as she raised her mouth to his. Her lips parted and clung in a kiss of stirring gentleness, a solemn pledge of their souls one to the other. Awed by the feel of his powerful body trembling at her touch and his tears of relief that she was safe, she murmered against his mouth, "I needed you so, Nick, and you came to me. I love you."

Nick kissed her with insatiable hunger, uncaring that they might be observed. Sudden realization of her injury made him pull away. "Forgive me. I didn't mean to hurt you, did I? You looked so fragile lying here that I had to assure myself that you were safe."

"You couldn't hurt me by touching . . . only by leaving."

Stroking her hair, Nick let the long strands glide through his fingers, thrilling to the feel of its texture against his skin. He inhaled the fragrance, the clean smell tantalizing his nostrils, before he placed his lips to it with yearning.

"Sit down by me, darling. That way I don't have to let go of you." Each desperate to talk, they spent the next few hours clearing up the misunderstanding that had nearly cost them their love. Her fingers wandered over his brow, the planes of his face, before outlining the shape of his firm mouth. Eyes filled with love, she trembled as he placed feathery kisses against her hand. "The doctor told me I can go home in four days and return to duty in about two months."

The sensuous feel of his circling tongue on her palm stopped as he raised his head to inform her adamantly, "You're mistaken about one thing, sweetheart. You will never return to work! My wife will have a full-time occupation satisfying me." His meaning clear, he kissed her sensitive inner wrist, feeling the increasing pulsebeat at his caress. "You can regale our children with your exploits as a big-city cop, but as of now you are my exclusive property. I will see that arrangements are made immediately to release you from your commitment to the City of Los Angeles. The sooner you turn in your badge the happier I'll be!"

Looking at his serious expression, Carlyn teased, "Arrogant man! Don't I have any say in the matter?"

Unabashed by her question, he retorted, "Not one whit!" His mouth molded hers in a fiery kiss that emphasized the solemnity of his declaration and told her more than words could of his need to keep her safely by his side from that time on. "That should convince you that I mean what I say. As much as I hate to leave you I must return to my business. When you're released, I'll come back and we'll fly to my home in northern California. You'll recuperate rapidly in beautiful Mendocino County, in the deep woods with lots of clean air." Stroking her wrist and slender arm sensuously, his eyes darkened from slate-gray to obsidian-black. His tightly checked emotions flared at the response visible in her velvety glance and the sudden trembling of her lips. "I can hardly wait to take care of you, to have you alone," he moaned, his voice slurred with passion.

Overwhelmed by Nick's ability to arouse her with a single glance, she pulled his sleek black head to her. Touching his lips, she inhaled the scent of his tangy after-shave before clasping him to her breast. The weight of his face against her body as she stroked his vibrant hair filled her heart with peace. "What will your neighbors think about you living with an unmarried lady?"

Reluctant to lift his head, he laughed. "I don't have any neighbors close enough to know. Besides, I intend to alter your single status as soon as I can arrange the wedding." Her breath fanned his mouth as he nibbled the corner of her lips, reminding her he did not intend to wait long for his bride.

"Nick"—she changed the subject abruptly—"hand me my purse."

As she withdrew an envelope from the zippered compartment, Nick recognized it instantly and flushed. "Can you ever forgive me for that horrible insult to you?" He took her in his arms and cradled her reverently. "That was unforgivable of me, despite my shock."

Cupping his face, she kissed him softly. "Would you consider letting me use the money to furnish a nursery?" she whispered shyly.

"Aren't propositioning me, are you?" he asked, sitting back in his chair, a frown of contemplation creasing his forehead.

"Definitely not, Nick. My career of propositioning men has ended!"

The jeopardy of her narrow escape filled him with sudden anger, and he tried to erase the fear from his mind. His great body shuddered, animosity violently spilling forth with each word. "Damn the police department, Carlyn. They used you! You were nothing to them but a sensuous decoy!"

"No, darling. I was a willing decoy. Now hush, please. I'm going to be fine. It was my job and one that I've always loved." She pleaded for his understanding.

Nick paced the small room, his emotions volatile, his darkened eyes glittering with sudden hatred. He said furiously, "It's a good thing that bastard died! I nearly killed him myself when I saw his hands on your waist, his cruel eyes filled with lust!"

Carlyn reached out for his hand in an attempt to soothe his anger. "Forget it, darling. Remembering all this sorrow and unhappiness can only bring us more pain."

Determined to placate her despite his wrath, he smiled. "About that nursery, *cara!* The picture of your body burgeoning with my child blows my mind, but I have a deep need within me, darling. An insatiable need for you alone. If you'll agree to one year with only the two of us, I'll fill a whole damn nursery for you!"

The thought of Carlyn arched beneath him in the aftermath of lovemaking was too much for Nick's control. "I must feel the length of your body against me." He enfolded her within his clasp and moaned in frustration, "What a miserable place to want to make love this room is. I can't even fit on the bed with you."

Nick's firm lips closed over her mouth, hungrily probing its moistness, feeling her tongue touch his in response. He kissed her with abandon, trying to shut out all memories of their turbulent misjudgment. Stopped by her murmurs of heightened pleasure, he released her mouth. With gentle hands he lay her on the pillow, stroking her tumbled hair, agonizingly aware of her heaving breasts.

"I love you, Nick," she whispered breathlessly, arms outstretched.

"Don't start with the magic again, please. You affect me so, that everytime I'm close I can't keep my hands or mouth off you. God, Carlyn, I hate to leave you but I have so many business problems."

Tears floooded her eyes as she sat up, stuttering plaintively, "I—I—I'll miss you, darling." She was filled with pain knowing he would soon leave.

Nick cradled her carefully in his strong grip as she rested her head against his chest, her arms tight around his neck. He felt sobs rack through her slim body; he stroked her back to console her, his hands sliding slowly over her spine. "One more kiss before I go, *mia cara*. I have to start work immediately if I'm going to take the next three months off. We'll have the entire summer in our mountain home." Taking her mouth in a searching kiss, he moaned, "I love you so." Their passionate kiss was interrupted by knocks on the door.

Linda, having been alerted by the nurse's aid that a seemingly very worried stranger had come to visit Carlyn, had had a gut feeling that the visitor was Nick. She had passed by Carlyn's room, peeked in and, seeing them in a warm embrace, knew she had guessed correctly. Now she knocked twice before entering the room.

"Time for lunch, Carlyn." She smiled at the happiness radiating between them. Nick's overpowering, handsome arrogance would be impossible for any young woman to resist, she thought as Carlyn introduced them. After adjusting the tray, she excused herself and left, amazed that Doug had contacted him so fast.

Disheartened at saying good-bye, Nick followed Nurse Sanderson out, mind intent on the multitude of business problems awaiting him.

An hour later, Carlyn's father, weary from his unsuccessful trip north, entered her room, his shoulders drooping in defeat. Doug was stunned to find himself greeted ecstatically, his daughter's face filled with exhilaration.

"Daddy, I'm so happy!" she exclaimed joyously. "I have so much to tell you. I'm in love with a man named Nick." Breathlessly she told him the entire story, as he stared into her sparkling eyes.

Hands raised in defeat after hearing her tale, he laughed. "Daughter dear, how you do go on about the man, but I must tell you I have traveled over twelve hundred miles to find this knight in shining armor. I found his gates locked, house firmly secured, and you have the nerve to tell me my trip was all in vain? Our paths must have crossed in midair." Anxious to meet Nick, he queried, "Where is he?"

Tears brimming her eyes, Carlyn wailed with unhappiness as she explained about Nick's business commitments. Then, in a lighter voice, "He's taking three months off from work to take care of me at his home up north."

"A beautiful home it is. Built by someone with love and understanding of the area's natural environment. I've never seen more magnificent trees outside a park. There's even a lake—undoubtedly stocked with fish waiting for me to catch them," he teased warmly.

"Nick designed and built it by himself, Daddy," she bragged.

Time passed slowly for Carlyn while waiting for Nick's return. Each day she felt stronger, more anxious to leave. Their daily phone calls were a torment, the need to be together a physical agony. By working day and night Nick told her he was clearing his desk of his most pressing problems. The others he would delegate to his managers.

On the day of Nick's arrival Linda, who had spent each evening with Doug since his return, helped Carlyn dress. She teased her, "Settle down, dear, or Doctor Hargrove will order you back to bed. He's still amazed at how much

194

faster you've improved since Nick's visit. It will be a few weeks till you're back to normal, but you shouldn't have any further difficulties. Remember, the bandage is water-proof in case you want to bathe tonight." Admiring Carlyn's ɪavender print dress with its flowing skirt and blouson top, she told her, "You're very beautiful, Carlyn. I wanted children badly and nothing would have made me more proud than having a daughter exactly like you."

Overwhelmed by Linda's words, Carlyn hugged her, thanking her for the compliment and telling her how much she would miss her.

With a shy smile Linda said, "I hope you don't mind my dating your father. He's a wonderful man and we enjoy each other's company. I never tire of hearing about his home in Oregon." Soft brown eyes shining with warmth, she questioned, "Has he told you he's staying in town for a few days after you leave the hospital? He's had several long conversations with Nick and feels your future is well taken care of. Doug wants to introduce me to some of his friends that he hasn't seen since he retired."

"I'm pleased," Carlyn told her honestly. "After the anguish I caused Daddy it's wonderful he can relax and enjoy part of his visit."

After Linda left, Carlyn stared out the window, hoping for a glimpse of Nick's car. She was so engrossed in her search for the Porsche that she didn't hear the door swing open.

She sensed Nick's presence at the same time he reached her. Just as she was about to turn she felt herself clasped from behind, his powerful arms holding her to the length of his strong body.

"I finally made it, darling," he whispered, his voice trembling with passion. Kissing her on the nape, he buried his face in the glory of her freshly shampooed hair, its perfumed fragrance heady in his nostrils. He turned her around and saw the love shining in her eyes. He cupped her breasts lovingly in his palms, his breath catching at the contact.

Carlyn's lips quivered as she sought his mouth. She felt herself reeling with the sweet taste of his ardent caress.

Nick splayed his fingers across her lower back, holding her firmly to the hardened contours of his aroused body. "Now do you feel how much I've missed you these last few days?" Smiling at the quick flush that tinged her cheeks from his obvious implication, he teased, "Come, my bashful bride-to-be. I'll take you to your apartment. Anything you can't part with for three months we'll take. I paid your rent through the summer, but I don't want to be bothered closing it up now."

"What an arrogant husband you're going to make, Mr. Sandini!" she laughed, lifting her chin haughtily. "I couldn't see your Porsche in the parking lot."

"Probably because I didn't drive it! I have a rented car today. You look like a greedy little minx so you might appreciate this." Laughing at her look of disbelief at his comment, he took a small velvet box from his suit pocket and handed it to her. "For such a little hunk of glass it sure cost me a bundle."

Tension mounted between them as she realized what it was. Breathless, she opened the velvet box. Nestled in burgundy satin a perfect solitaire reflected brilliant fire. The huge oval diamond stunned her, magnificent in its broad gold setting. Speechless with emotion, she stared at the perfection of her ring, tears trickling down her face.

Nick took the ring, raised her left hand, and slipped it on her third finger. As her hand trembled he kissed it tenderly before turning her palm upward to place a kiss in the center. Closing her fingers, he looked deeply into her yearning eyes. His voice, husky with the depth of his feelings, caressed her. "Handle that with care, my darling. Your palm holds my heart, my love, and my life."

She placed her hands on his nape and raised on tiptoes to kiss him, slowly giving him her own pledge of love.

Tasting the salt of her tears on his tongue, he pulled away. "It's not cheap chartering an airplane. Your kissing will cost me overtime!"

"Since I will soon have a legal right to share your fortune, I'd better start conserving it," she teased mischievously.

"Insolent minx!" he scolded, giving her a firm slap on the rear before escorting her into the hall.

As she saw her father standing near the nurses station, she grabbed Nick's hand, tugging him with her as she proudly showed her engagement ring. "I'll miss you, Daddy," she cried sadly. "Promise to visit us on your way home. Nick said he'd let you fish," she added as an unneeded incentive. Hugging him tightly, she was conscious of the fact that she was entering another phase of her life: the time in her life when a man other than her father sought her love. "Will I see you soon?"

"Maybe sooner than you think, daughter dear," he told her, glancing over the top of her silky hair at Nick. "Now be on your way." Pushing her toward Nick, his feelings tightly checked, he teased, "You'll have your hands full with this one, Nick. She's been dreadfully spoiled by her brother and me for many years now."

Nick pulled her to him possessively and rubbed Carlyn's shoulders intimately. Looking Doug in the eye, he told him seriously, "I have a feeling she will coerce me into continuing the bad habit, and I'll end up loving every minute, besides." Glancing at his watch, Nick reminded her that they had to leave. Amidst hugs, kisses, and tears they left the hospital, anxious to leave the memory of the last few dreadful weeks behind them.

Most of her luggage had been thoughtfully packed by Marianne beforehand so it took only thirty minutes to gather her things in her apartment. At the airport Carlyn followed in amazement as Nick led her up the ramp into the interior of a large airplane. Welcomed aboard by the attractive flight attendants, they were seated in the front compartment. Sitting next to the window, she felt Nick lower his large frame into the adjoining seat.

As she fastened her seat belt for takeoff he looked at her with concern. "How are you feeling, sweetheart? Are you tired or in pain?"

Her hand clasping his, she looked into his keen gray eyes filled with solicitude. "I feel fine, although I didn't expect to fly in a plane this size. You didn't charter the entire jet just to take me north, did you?" she inquired curiously.

"I did." he replied adamantly. "I didn't want to waste time traveling, and this cruises around four hundred and fifty miles per hour. Our flight will be about seventy-five minutes, so relax and shut your eyes."

Feeling tense, she held Nick's hand tightly when the plane quivered from the force of its powerful jet engines. The whining noise was a vibrating drone to her sensitive ears as they taxied along the runway. Nick's indifference was that of a man used to commuting around the world and helped calm her anxiety. She enjoyed the view of Los Angeles as they lifted smoothly into the pale blue sky. Gaining altitude rapidly, the aircraft banked as it circled north.

The steady hum of the jet engines lulled Carlyn into a state of euphoria, and she leaned against the tall seat. Nick, relaxing beside her, gripped her fingers firmly in his lean hand. An unruly wave of ebony hair fell forward over his forehead. Unable to resist the temptation, Carlyn smoothed it lovingly, the touch causing her pulse to beat erratically.

Turning sideways, Nick held her gaze. "I love you, darling. Tonight for the first time we won't have to part," he whispered suggestively, placing a searing kiss in the palm of her hand.

She smiled softly at him, eyes darkening with passion and love.

"Don't look at me like that. I don't think you want to shock our flight attendants, do you? The sensual invitation in your eyes demands reciprocation, so ease the tension a little and gaze at the view. It's safer for you and easier on me. My days of taking cold showers are over and we're a long way from your new home."

Obedient to his suggestion, she watched the cumulus clouds pass below and the sudden emergence of the snow-capped Sierra Nevada Mountains. After the plane had descended and was taxiing to a smooth landing, Carlyn looked at Nick in a quandary. "Where are we?"

"You'll find out where and why as soon as you stand up." Nick assisted her from her seat and, with a hand on her forearm, guided her to the rear compartment of the plane.

Astounded, Carlyn stared with wide eyes at her father, brother, Marianne, Linda, Captain Stinson, Tim, George, Ralph, and Dr. Masters, who Carlyn met for the first time. The men wore formal suits and Linda and Marianne were dressed to the teeth in elegant gowns.

Unaware of the significance of the entourage, Carlyn gazed mesmerized at their smiling faces before leaning gratefully against Nick for support. His breath fanning her ear, he explained with amusement, "This is our wedding party, sweetheart."

As everyone shouted their greetings Carlyn froze, for a moment too dazed to talk. "I can't believe it." Staring at Linda, she exclaimed, "You were in uniform only two hours ago!" Turning to her father, she shook her head. "Now I understand why you were at the hospital. You came to pick up Linda." She turned to Nick, her violet eyes shining with happiness and astonishment, as she wailed plaintively, "I don't have anything to wear! Everyone but me is dressed formal—and I'm the bride!"

"Complaining about the lack of clothes already and we're not even married. She really is spoiled, Doug," he teased, smiling at her father. "I'll make her wait until we get to the chapel for her next surprise. Come on, everyone, I'm an impatient bridegroom."

All talking at once, laughing at the raucous teasing, they left the plane and entered the waiting chauffeured limousines hired to drive them to their Reno, Nevada, destination.

Taken into a private room by Linda and Marianne a shaking Carlyn was shown her wedding gown for the first time. Tears of joy came to her eyes as she gazed with wonderment at her elegant hand-sewn gown as Linda removed it from its protective wrapper.

Yards of white chiffon and handmade lace, it was exquisitely styled with a high Victorian collar and buttoned front accented by a V-shaped ruffle over the bodice and at the wrists of the long sleeves. With it was a short veil and wispy lace bra and panty set. Marianne held up a satin garter belt for the filmy hose and dainty white satin slippers to complete her outfit.

Overwhelmed with happiness, she could hardly wait to try on her dress. Linda checked her bandaged side before helping her button her gown and placing the lacy veil over her lustrous hair. The sweet perfume of fresh orange blossoms filled the room as Marianne added a tiny coronet to the band of her veil.

Standing before the full-length mirror, Carlyn thought it amazing that the starry-eyed girl was her own reflection. Linda handed her a pale blue satin garter and Carlyn pulled it over her right thigh, thanking her as she took a small lace hanky from Marianne. "I'm ready now. Something borrowed and something blue." A sharp knock reminded them time was limited.

Linda opened the door, smiling at Doug before standing aside so he could view his lovely daughter. He handed her a bouquet of white orchids, tears shimmering in his eyes as he solemnly looked at her beloved face.

With a grave expression he stared at her for a moment, then bent to place a kiss on her smooth cheek. "You are a beautiful bride, Carlyn. Nick is a very lucky man to be receiving the most precious gift a father can give his future son-in-law." Observing her radiant eyes bright with unshed tears, he smiled and hugged her to his broad chest. "No tears, please. It's time for me to take you to your restless bridegroom."

Placing her right hand over his arm, he proudly escorted her up the aisle. Somber sounds of "The Wedding March" filled the small room as she walked regally beside her distinguished gray-haired father.

Nick towered over the other men as he stood waiting, his formal black suit, immaculate shirt, and silk tie a perfect foil for his darkly handsome looks. His gray eyes darkened, the smoldering look of passion tightly checked visible in their depths, as he watched the graceful movements of Carlyn coming toward him.

Thank you, God, for leading me to the other half of my heart, she prayed silently as she walked down the aisle.

At the altar Doug turned to his daughter, lifted her blusher veil, and placed a gentle kiss on her smooth cheek. He shook Nick's hand earnestly, then stepped aside as the minister began to pronounce the age-old rite. Nick and Carlyn were married in a short but emotional ceremony, joining their lives through eternity.

Nick's hands shook as he placed the heavy gold band on Carlyn's finger before giving her a matching band to place on his. He cupped her face in his palms, awed by her teary eyes. They were unaware of their watching friends: their gazes locked for a long tension-filled moment before Nick lowered his head. Her lips were trembling as they exchanged their first kiss as man and wife. He lifted his face with reluctance from her responsive mouth, and they were barraged with congratulations, grains of rice, and eager men anxious to kiss the deliriously enraptured bride.

His strong arm possessively around Carlyn's shoulders, Nick raised his other hand to stop them. "I told you I would fly you to Reno for the wedding, but I didn't say I'd let you stay here long enough to kiss my bride," he informed them decisively.

Nick's ribald bantering was taken with good humor, and the wedding party was soon boarding the chartered plane. Nick's foresight once again stunned Carlyn as she ducked through the streamers that decorated the interior. Silver wedding bells hung from the ceiling, placed there by the flight attendants during the ceremony. Her mind whirled with thoughts of her dynamic bridegroom, realizing she had married a man who could accomplish the impossible if he so desired.

Motioning with his hand, Nick told the guests to sit in the forward section for the return flight and to keep their seat belts fastened for at least ten minutes. "That's how long it will take to give my wife a proper kiss."

After they were seated in the aft of the plane, he turned her to him. With gentle hands he embraced her shoulders, his glance lingering on the loveliness of her face, the beauty of her uniquely colored eyes.

Yearning for his touch, she turned to place a kiss on his hand.

"Kiss me, wife!" he commanded, his voice lowering as he inhaled the perfumed scent of her hair and skin. He felt her lips cling as he kissed her with intense satisfaction, his hands cupping her face firmly.

Steel-hard muscles tightened beneath her hands as she returned each kiss, passionately aroused by the sound of his low voice whispering Italian words of love. It didn't matter that she couldn't speak the language, his meaning was transferred with each ardent touch and sensual caress.

Nick's breath brushed Carlyn's mouth, his voice a harsh murmur. "This is our appetizer." He covered her smooth cheeks with feathery kisses, tasting the salt of tears against his tongue. "Did I hurt you, *cara?*" he moaned, watching as they slowly ran down her face.

Thick lashes spiked with teardrops lowered as she shook her head no. "These are tears of happiness." Examining each contour of his striking face, she touched the corner of his mouth, tracing its outline while he nibbled her finger playfully. "I don't think I'll be able to breath if you kiss me one more time. You're too much."

"I haven't started yet!" His palm raised to her breast. The pounding of her heart, her responsiveness as she leaned closer, told him of her excitement. He placed a searing kiss on her throat before removing his hand and leaning against his own seat. "It's just as well our flight is short. This plane goes back to Los Angeles with our friends, while we board a smaller aircraft for the final journey home. I insist that our first night together will be in the mountains."

Dazed, she shook her head. "I can't keep up with you. You have everything arranged down to the smallest detail."

"Of course! I've arranged a wedding dinner at my Beverly Hills restaurant for our wedding guests and their families. A wedding dinner for everyone but us. Our dinner will be alone!"

"Time's up!" the others called in unison as they clambered down the aisle to the rear of the plane.

The attendants wheeled a cart holding a small three-tiered cake and ice-filled buckets of rare champagne to the joyous group. Nick nibbled her fingers as she held a slice of cake to his mouth; she giggled with delight as he fed her the small piece he had cut. The ornate swirls of frosting roses and doves were soon indistinguishable and the ceramic bride and groom that had adorned the top now rested on the cart. Their in-flight reception was cut short when the plane neared San Francisco, where Nick and Carlyn planned to depart.

Hugging her father, she was clasped firmly in his hearty grasp as he told her solemnly, "You and Nick will be very happy. You have that same capacity for giving that your mother had. It is a rare and cherished gift for any man to receive."

Standing on tiptoes, she kissed the rugged lines in his face. "Come see us soon."

Bob placed a fond kiss on her cheek, telling her he thought Nick made an excellent addition to their family.

Temporarily alone, she walked to Dr. Masters, knowing instantly why Nick considered him to be his best friend. He was much like Nick in size, and he had intelligent eyes that stared at her keenly. Taking her hand, he held it as he held her gaze. "Never doubt Nick's love, Carlyn. You have it all. His heart has never been shared with another, and he will be a faithful, loving husband. I can understand now the shock Nick must have felt seeing you in the hotel lounge. It's inconceivable that you could ever live a deceitful, promiscuous life."

After hugging Marianne and Linda, she handed her wedding bouquet to Linda, teasing her with the symbolism of receiving it, amused by her flushed cheeks and covert glance at Doug.

Captain Stinson, George, Ralph, and Tim crowded around her, telling her how happy they were for her, agreeing unanimously taking a special day off for her wedding was an experience they wouldn't have missed for the world.

Taking her slender shoulders in his capable hands Tim gazed at her with eyes barely suppressing the love he felt. "Best of everything, Carlyn. You deserve it. I like to think

I would have been the man for you, but after meeting Nick, I realize why I never stood a chance. It takes a special man to satisfy a very special lady." Hands trembling at the feel of her shapely body in his arms for the first and last time, he told her huskily, "I'm going to get that kiss you'd never give me though. Remember, if that brute of a husband ever gets out of line, he'll have the entire L.A.P.D. Ad. Vice Division to contend with!" Drawing her close, he kissed her fiercely on the lips, reluctantly lifting his head to stop his own response. His mind reeled with envy of Nick—envy at the thought that he would possess the woman Tim wanted more than any he had ever known.

Nick's eyes narrowed jealously as he placed a hand at Carlyn's waist and drew her from Tim's hold. Aware of the other man's feelings for his bride, he found it unbearable to allow even a parting kiss to linger between them.

Careful not to hurt her side, Nick guided Carlyn down the ramp and to the waiting twin-engine passenger plane. They glanced back briefly and gave a final wave to their friends watching from the windows of the large aircraft.

A wave of tiredness rushed over Carlyn as Nick helped her into the comfortable seat of the luxurious private plane. Relaxing, she let the feeling of lassitude overcome her. She snuggled next to him, resting her head on Nick's broad shoulder, her silvery hair spreading over the dark cloth of his suit in dazzling contrast.

CHAPTER FOURTEEN

Carlyn woke as the plane taxied to a stop at a private airstrip. Revived by her short nap, she took Nick's hand and ducked before stepping down the metal stairs. She felt at home the minute he seated her in the familiar Porsche. As she watched eagerly out the front window the coastal scenery flew by as Nick sped toward his home.

After unlocking the heavy metal entrance gate, he drove forward, then stopped to secure it behind him. "That should keep everyone out." He trailed his hand intimately up the side of her leg until she placed his fingers back on the steering wheel.

Aware of the sudden desire that fired her blood, Carlyn teased playfully, "Are you an isolationist, Nick?"

"My darling wife, with you in my arms I may never leave this property again!"

Nick lowered the windows so Carlyn could inhale the pungent aroma of his heavily forested property. The late-afternoon sun shone in long golden streaks of light through the feathery needles of rough-barked redwoods. Leafy ferns grew profusely on the spongy woodland floor. "This is the loveliest sight I have ever seen," she exclaimed, her rapturous face glowing with pleasure as she looked around.

Nick smiled tenderly, his mind at peace realizing his wife shared with him his deep love for nature's abundant beauty. The road dipped abruptly into a grassy valley before edging a large pond that shimmered startling emerald-green and was kept filled year round by a gurgling stream. After rounding a curve, he parked behind his mountain retreat. Nick's home stood tall and proud in its forest setting, welcoming Carlyn with warmth and beauty.

Overwhelmed by the elegance of the rugged hand-carved deck railing and the craftsmanship of the redwood exterior, she exclaimed, "I expected a log cabin and you bring me to a work of art in a picture-postcard setting." As she turned to him her eyes glimmered with happiness. "I love it already. Did you really build it yourself?"

"I most certainly did," he retorted arrogantly. "Every nail, every cut, was made by my hands. It took me over two years but it was a labor of love from the beginning. Wait until you see inside."

Inhaling the scent of pine needles and redwood, she was admiring the casual landscaping when Nick grabbed her and swung her into his arms. She was carried, squealing with delight, in all her wedding finery up the wide steps to the deck above.

Without releasing her, he turned toward the west. "Now look way down there. Isn't that gorgeous?"

Clinging to his strong neck, she gazed at the distant rugged coastline with its awe-inspiring allure.

Kissing her on the side of the face, he whispered seductively. "Our bedroom overlooks the same view from the upper deck." He blew softly against her ear as he teased, "You'll see more from that room than from this deck the first year or two!" Nick unlocked the heavy carved door and kicked it open to carry his bride over the threshold.

He set her down and lowered his head to her parted lips,

kissing her with hunger and need tightly held in check. His grip slackened as a shudder of intense desire raged through him. "I'm sorry. I keep forgetting that you just checked out of the hospital, but it's unbearable to keep my hands off you. Come on and look over your new home."

She was entranced by the quality and taste shown in its construction and decoration, and her eyes shone as she looked at Nick. "This is magnificent, darling. I like the open plan of the front room. I'll be able to watch you while I try out all those beautiful copper-colored appliances in the kitchen. Did you carve those posts that divide the two rooms?"

"Of course! I also made the maple cupboards, laid the gold ceramic tile on the counter and bar, fit the tiles on the kitchen floor, laid each used brick in the fireplace, built the bookcases on each side of it, and polished, waxed, varnished, stained, and painted the whole damn thing! I didn't build the furniture, make the windowpanes, or cut the shingles. Anything else, my sweet?"

Chuckling at his attitude of male superiority, she leaned on his shoulder as her eyes swept the room. "Your couch and lounge chairs are big enough for a giant." After she admired the soft fur throw rugs, she pulled Nick into the kitchen, her curiosity insatiable.

"Our kitchen is stocked with enough food to last us the full three months," he said, leering at her mischievously before opening a full-size pantry crammed with an assortment of grocery items and another cupboard with a filled canted wine rack. Snooping in the refrigerator and freezer, she felt a firm swat on her buttocks.

"It's time to see the most important room in the house."

"But I'm in it," she chuckled as he lifted her into his arms to ascend the wide stairway leading to the upper floor.

"I didn't mean the kitchen, and you know it." His eyes

shone as he heard her gasp of pleasure when he opened the door.

"Let me down. I want to explore every inch. This isn't just a bedroom, it's a private suite." Her eyes swung from the beamed ceiling, over the king-size bed, to the west wall, made entirely of glass.

Satin shoes sinking into the plush carpeting, she walked around the room before peeking into the bathroom. It was as big as most bedrooms. Its walls were varnished red-wood, skylights dotted the ceiling, and a full-length glass wall brushed the feathery fronds of the trees alongside the house. The center of attention was the mammoth-size marble tub, its oval shape matching that of the twin sinks. "Oh, dear."

Nick's laughter filled the room as he stood behind her. "Yes, my lovely, it will hold two comfortably, although it has not to date," he teased, reading her thoughts correctly. "Downstairs there are two more bedrooms with their own baths for our guests, but this entire top floor is our private domain."

"Can I take a bath, Nick?" she asked, suddenly weary.

"Of course, darling. I'll get the luggage, then fix us a light dinner. I haven't eaten anything all day except that tasteless white wedding cake." He drew her forward, hugging her gently, his chin resting on her shiny hair. "Why are wedding cakes always white? I would have much preferred chocolate."

Pressed against the hard wall of his broad chest, she laughed softly. "You're crazy. A three-tiered chocolate cake sounds awful."

"Tastes better though," he grumbled, his hands caressing her back. "There are plenty of all those woman things in the medicine chest. Marianne told me all your favorite scents and I had them delivered along with the groceries."

Thrilled at his continued thoughtfulness, she thanked him, watching as he left to get their luggage. She filled the deep tub, adding a generous capful of bubble bath, anxious to soak in the relaxing warmth.

Wanting to take a last look at the ocean before the sun set, Carlyn walked to the window. She watched, entranced by the natural beauty, as Nick set their luggage down and came to her.

Drawing her against him, he turned her into his arms, his keen eyes reading the sudden doubt in her mind. "Don't be frightened, darling. I'm aware how tired you are. To have you safe in my care is enough for me now." As he kissed her forehead his breath fanned the silken waves of hair, the warmth causing her to lean into the comfort of his strong body. "Now, my love, let me have the pleasure of removing your wedding gown."

"I can do it, Nick," she said, walking away from him.

"Come here, darling, and be still," he commanded as she glanced over her shoulder.

Smiling impudently at him, she obeyed. "If I want any dinner, I'd better listen to you this time. Of course when I'm fit, it will be another story." She stopped before him, her eyes bright with love.

"We'll see about that, wife." Cupping her face in his palms, he placed his mouth over hers in a gentle kiss that only hinted at the passion to come.

Nick's hands lowered, and with deft fingers he undid each tiny button on the front of her gown. He ran his hands lightly up her arms and eased the gown over her shoulders. Carlyn bowed her head, her thick sooty lashes hiding the surgence of love visible in her eyes. She trembled when he eased the bodice carefully down to her waist and, holding it with one hand, cupped her breast with the other. The warmth of his gentle fingers against her swelling breast brought a flush to her face that matched the fiery response of her body. She watched, hypnotized, as he lowered his head, felt him trail a searing kiss from the wildly pulsating hollow of her throat to the edge of her lacy bra.

He let the gown fall in a filmy cloud of chiffon around her feet. As he stared at her shapely body clad in the lacy underwear, his eyes narrowed, gray absorbed by black as his pupils dilated. Sitting on the end of his wide bed he pulled her between his knees as he looked at the bandage above her slender waist. "Let me see where that bitch shot you."

"I can't, Nick. I'm not supposed to remove the tape today." Uneasy at standing before him in her brief underwear, she squirmed, her face flushing a soft rose.

Clasping her hips, his broad hands spanned them easily as he pulled her forward, his head lowering until his lips touched her side. He raised his face to look at her. "Now that I've kissed your side it will heal better." Touching her garter, he smiled. "That's a rather enticing but useless article." His hands kneaded the soft flesh of her hips as he leaned forward to trail a series of burning kisses across her smooth abdomen. As his tongue circled her navel she grasped his dark head with trembling fingers. Her stomach muscles clenched spasmodically, and her legs threatened to collapse beneath her.

He looked up, breaking contact reluctantly, his smoldering eyes locking with her frightened gaze. Nick stood up and pulled Carlyn into his arms, unable to resist pressing her to the hardened contours of his aroused body. "If we're going to have any dinner, I'd better leave you now."

She arched her body and wound her arms around his nape, feeling his mouth caress the side of her neck in a series of urgent kisses. "God, Carlyn, you could drive a man wild with your delectable body. My weeks of celibacy have my control teetering on razor-sharp edge." He turned her around and slapped her playfully on her shapely buttocks.

Carlyn strode to the bathroom and, glancing over her

shoulder, chuckled at his tense expression and tightly clenched hands. She suggested mischievously, "You're too much for me to handle. Did you ever think of getting a television?"

His voice raised as she shut the door, his quick retort a warning. "My idea of interesting entertainment travels along a different path, as you will soon find out." Her laughter followed him down the stairs.

Carlyn lay back in the soothing warmth of the water. Holding her hand to the light, she admired the fiery diamond and wide gold band so heavy on her finger. The tension and stiffness in her limbs left as she relaxed in the scented foam and closed her eyes in deep repose.

Nick's entrance roused her from her lethargy. She remained still.

"Time's up, honey. You'll get chilled if you stay in there much longer. I've already fixed dinner and showered." Bending, Nick raised the lever releasing the water in an eddy. Clasping her arms, he pulled her upward and ran his hands over her sleek wet body before wrapping her in the soft bathsheet. Telling her to stand still, he gently rubbed every inch of her flushed skin dry as if it were the most natural thing in the world.

Carlyn tried desperately to control her shyness at the unaccustomed feel of a man's hands on her naked body. She tensed as his touch became more intimate.

Sensing her embarrassment, Nick held her hands, his hypnotic voice reassuring her, "Never feel ashamed at me seeing or touching any part of you. I adore every satiny inch!"

A loving smile touched his lips as he rewrapped Carlyn in the soft towel, his nostrils flaring at her heady scent. "I'll bring up our dinner while you get dressed."

Opening her suitcase, Carlyn found a creamy satin and lace nightgown with matching peignoir wrapped in tissue paper. Tears shimmered in her eyes at the thoughtfulness

212

of Bob and Marianne as she read the tender note attached to their gift.

The sleek gown fell in smooth folds around her hips, its lace top plunging in a deep décolletage. Uncomfortable with the vast amount of naked breast exposed, Carlyn pulled the peignoir over her arms. She sat on the edge of the bed and brushed her hair until it fell in gleaming waves around her shoulders.

She stood when Nick entered the room, carrying a large tray. "Umm . . . that smells heavenly," Carlyn complimented him, enjoying the smell of spicy spaghetti sauce.

"So do you. The perfume of your body makes meat and mushroom sauce seem pretty mundane." He set their plates on a small oval table near the glass wall, adding silverware and napkins before placing a single candle in the center of the table. The flame flickered romantically in the darkened room as Nick switched off the overhead light.

Seated at the cozy table, Carlyn smiled, appreciative of the delicious-looking meal cooked by her husband. "I'm suddenly starving. Anything else for me?" she teased, watching in surprise as Nick left the room. Her eyes widened as he returned in a moment, carrying a silver ice bucket that held a bottle of champagne and a single crystal goblet.

His eyes lingered on the beauty of her negligee as he sat opposite her at the table. "I'd rather feast on you, Carlyn," he teased.

Laughing at his foolishness, she took a bite of sauce. Thoughtfully she cocked her head, her expression bland. "Not bad." Pursing her lips, she teased, "Of course after hospital food for a week, anything would taste good."

"Ungrateful wretch," he scolded.

"Would you feel better if I told you in all sincerity that you are the best cook in the world? Your father must be a fantastic person to have taught you so well." Her eyes

213

widened as she looked at Nick. "My gosh, I completely forgot about your parents. Do they know we're married?"

"Yes, they know their son has finally been caught and they're truly thrilled. I promised them I would take you to Italy and introduce you to all your new relatives after our honeymoon. But not even the thought of seeing my parents will cause me to cut short our time alone. Have you traveled much, sweetheart?"

"Not outside the United States. I've always wanted to though."

"My dear wife, before our first year of marriage is complete, I will have escorted you anywhere in the world your heart desires."

Continually amazed by the generosity of her husband, she pushed her plate aside. She took a final sip of champagne from their single shared glass, then sighed wearily.

Rising, Nick gathered their plates, returning to the kitchen with the remains of their uneaten meal.

As she turned back the plain quilted spread she looked with longing at the chocolate-brown and beige-trimmed satin sheets.

When Nick returned from clearing the kitchen, he found his wife propped against a fluffy pillow, her gleaming hair and creamy gown vivid against the dark bed linens. He handed her a refilled glass of champagne, then sat on the edge of the bed, silent, his mood serious as he watched the candle flicker. He took the glass from her hand and set it down before reaching forward. "Mrs. Nicholas Sandini, your husband would like a kiss before tucking you in bed for the night."

Eager for his caress, she reached to enfold him, soft lips parted in anticipation.

"You smell heavenly, darling," he whispered huskily. He bent to her, purposely avoiding her lips to kiss the side of her neck. Nibbling on the sensitive skin, he moved upward, his tongue probing around the pink lobe and inner ear. His breath fanned her as he whispered, "Place your hand on my heart and feel how much I love you."

His shoulder muscles tensed as she slid her hands across the breadth of his chest. Slipping her fingers beneath the open neckline of his shirt, she ran them through the thick hair that covered his heart. Its rapid beat caused her own senses to respond, arousing the desire to touch him. She let her fingers trail downward, caressing each finely defined muscle as she unbuttoned his shirt.

His breath, playing across her cheek and inner ear, was erratic as her hands stroked his body. He rained hot, hungry kisses along the side of her neck and the hollow of her creamy shoulder, avoiding the temptation to seize her mouth.

Moaning, her heart pounding with desire, Carlyn pulled back from his arousing touch. "Kiss me properly, Nick, please."

Responding instantly, he moved his mouth over her cheek to her waiting lips. His tongue probed sensuously as he kissed her, his body trembling when he felt her responding touch. He felt tension mount between them as he began the unhurried seduction of his innocent bride. Tender, coaxing fingers fondled her shoulders as he ravished her mouth in a searing kiss.

Tortured by the shattering pleasure of his touch, her body throbbed with desire, her awakening passions suddenly inflamed. She felt shocked by her own response as she clung to him when he attempted to draw away. Her slumberous eyes pleaded as he removed his lips from her mouth. The look in his eyes heightened her desire. Poignantly she begged without shame, "Make love to me, darling. I can't bear another night of not belonging to you." As she let her supple body arch toward him, it made an irresistible appeal.

He stood abruptly, his muscles tense, fists tightly clenched. His eyes slid over her slender body. Her full breasts strained the lace of her bodice as they rose and fell with her tumultuous breathing. "Do you realize what you're asking? I've been too long without your touch. You're surely aware that your first experience may be painful and not bring you the pleasure I can give you when I have awakened you fully. Besides, you've just come from the hospital."

"Let me give myself to you, Nick," she cried passionately, her body aching for his touch. "I'm fine, really I am."

Lowering himself to the bed, he took her hands. "Raise up, sweetheart, so I can remove your gown. I want nothing between us now." As she lay back against the sheets, naked, he thought her the most beautiful woman in the world. His eyes lingered on the perfection of each curve of her body. The fire in his glance caused her nerves to tingle with burning expectation.

"Let me see your body, Nick. I want to touch you and feel the length of you against me." She watched as he stood and undressed with a casualness that eased the last of her anxiety. The strength of his body, the rippling muscles across wide shoulders, his tanned skin with its thick mat of hair veeing down his chest, his flat abdomen, and his aroused manhood caused her breath to catch in expectation. His narrow hips and long sinewy legs were symmetrically perfect, each muscle sculpted and magnificent in its masculinity.

She raised to meet him as their bodies joined on the wide bed. The feel of his steel-hard limbs, his heaving chest against her breasts, and his clinging mouth brought each nerve ending in her body to life. As his hands wandered freely over her shape she let her innate femininity guide her own hands to those sensitive areas that would bring him the most pleasure, as eager to touch as to be touched.

Nick cupped her engorged breast in his palm and lowered his head to the erect tip. Hungry for the taste of her skin, he circled the sensitive nipple with his flicking tongue, his warm mouth moist as it surged against her creamy curves.

Carlyn moved rhythmically beneath him, her passionate murmurs of pleasure torturing his self-control. Her fingers dug into his shoulders and trembled as she strained upward.

With erotic nibbles he trailed his mouth around her breasts, then left the enticement of her hardened nipples to drift downward. Intent on caressing every inch of her delectable body, he slid his lips across her rib cage to her quivering stomach. He covered her abdomen with reverent kisses, his restless hands continuing to stroke the velvety skin of her thighs.

Patient, knowing how to give her pleasure, he slid his long fingers gently along her inner thigh to part her legs.

Carlyn's legs clenched in sudden embarrassment, and she started to rise, to stop the intimacy of his hands.

"No, Nick. . . ."

His mouth continued to move across her soft stomach, careful to avoid hurting her bandaged side. "Yes . . . everywhere!" he commanded in a husky voice.

She grasped his hand as it rested possessively on her feminine hair, a sudden feeling of sensual inadequacy making her body tense.

"Don't stop me, *mia cara*. Let me show you how beautiful touching can be. How exquisite it feels."

A shiver of ecstasy ran through her at his insistent touch. Unable to deny her body's response, she lay back, pliant to his continued manipulation of her senses.

With each unhurried stroke he explored the hidden recesses of her virtuous body. The motion of his restless hand as he intimately caressed her, along with the torture of his wandering mouth as it descended to seek its final pleasure, brought a poignant cry from deep in her throat.

"Oh, Nick darling . . . not there!"

"Especially there." His naked shoulders shone in the

dim candlelight as he worshiped her with his mouth. "Oh, God, *mia cara*. You're beautiful. So . . . so innocent."

"Nick . . . please . . . umm!" she moaned as wave after wave of pleasure filled her body.

"Please. Please what? Tell me what you want."

Breathless at the warmth of his mouth following the pulsating touch of his fingers, she lay trembling, on fire with the instinctive feminine need to be possessed by the man she loved. Her emotions were no longer in control. Arching her hips, she began to move sensually, her voice pleading for release from his mouth.

"I want you, Nick. Oh, darling . . . please love me now!"

Knowing Carlyn was ready for the culmination of their love, Nick pulled her into the curve of his body, his chest rubbing sensually against her swollen breasts. A damp sheen of perspiration covered his broad back as he moved to claim her as his wife.

He whispered against her ear, "With my body I thee worship." Her searing response stretched his control to the limits, but he waited until she could feel the maximum pleasure.

With a shudder Carlyn clung, feeling wave after wave of warmth fill her body. Her tensions were released in one final burst of earth-shattering ecstasy—ecstasy Nick had never reached and Carlyn was unaware existed.

With kittenlike strokes Carlyn kneaded Nick's back, her bruised mouth raining kisses on his neck while he continued to hold her tenderly to his body. Her mind reeled with the bliss of his lovemaking, the seductive sound of his whispered love-words as he enveloped her in a glow of contentment. Totally relaxed, she stretched her limbs languorously before drifting into a deep sleep.

Nick's arms continued to hold her possessively, her slender body molded comfortably to his warmth. The candle flickered and died, leaving the room in darkness while they slept, fulfilled and momentarily appeased.

Before dawn he awoke to the excitement of Carlyn's pliant body curled sensuously to his contours. Instantly responsive to a burning kiss on the side of her throat, she turned. Clinging to his naked shoulders, she trailed soft kisses across his jaw.

As she felt his body harden against her she snuggled closer into his arms and murmured sleepily, "Mmm . . . that was so nice." She glided her hands across his shoulders, eager to experience the joy of his possession again.

His lips searched her neck, her perfumed skin as familiar as his own scent to him now. His desire undimmed by their first coming together, he questioned tenderly, "Did I hurt you, honey? I tried to be gentle with you, but you felt so good beneath me." His hands rubbed the satiny skin of her back before drawing her closer. "Feel what you do to me?"

"Yes." Running her smooth leg over his calf, she admitted, "I never knew it could be like that, Nick. I thought I'd die, it was so . . . so beautiful with you."

"You better lie still or you'll find out right now that it can be even better for you the second time."

"Promises, promises," she teased, deliberately moving against him as her lips raised to seek his mouth.

"Hush, wench." His mouth took hers in a fiery kiss. Their love too new and not easily satiated, they slowly brought each other to a shattering summit of rapture that surpassed their first encounter.

A passionate and virile man, Nick had a strong need for his beloved wife. A need that was satisfied eagerly by Carlyn's unending love for her husband. The gray light of early dawn streaked the sky as they made love, their bodies joining once more before they slept, both languorous after the unhurried coupling.

The sun was high overhead when they awoke the second time. Nick and Carlyn took a leisurely shower together before walking arm in arm to their bedroom's picture window high on the mountainside. His hands were gentle, his touch possessive, as he cradled her naked body. He put his lips to her brow in a tender kiss, his heart pounding at the dreamy look of love in her darkened eyes.

"This is where I wanted you from the first moment we met, my sensuous decoy. Umm . . . seems that I owe you three thousand dollars now."

Her tumbled hair vivid against his tanned shoulder, she leaned into him, instinctively seeking his warmth and strength. With her head tilted and a mischievous smile tugging her lips, she teased, "It's a good thing you're a very wealthy man, then, because as virile as you are, I'd have your entire fortune before the first year's up."

Nick swatted her indignantly on her buttocks, and she went, laughing, into his arms, clinging to his waist, her face tight against his hair-covered chest. Her voice was muffled as she nuzzled him unashamedly.

"Guess I'd better give you a free lifetime pass, because by the feel of your body I'm soon to be earning my fourth thousand-dollar bill!"

Their laughter filled the room as Nick swung Carlyn into his arms and carried her back to the tumbled covers on the bed still filled with the warmth of their love.

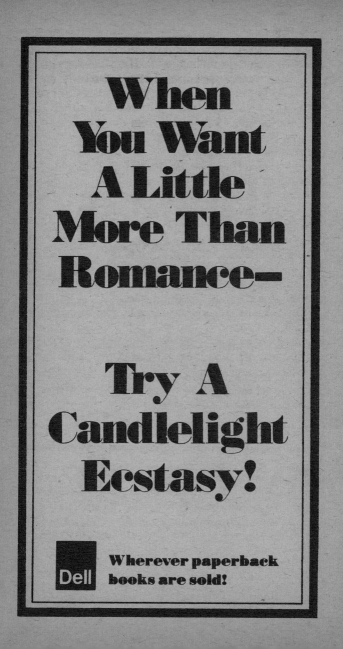

The second volume in the spectacular Heiress series

The Cornish Heiress

by Roberta Gellis
bestselling author of
The English Heiress

Meg Devoran—by night the flame-haired smuggler, Red Meg. Hunted and lusted after by many, she was loved by one man alone...

Philip St. Eyre—his hunger for adventure led him on a desperate mission into the heart of Napoleon's France.

From midnight trysts in secret smugglers' caves to wild abandon in enemy lands, they pursued their entwined destinies to the end—seizing ecstasy, unforgettable adventure—and love.

A Dell Book   **$3.50**   **(11515-9)**

VOLUME I IN THE EPIC NEW SERIES

The Morland Dynasty

The FOUNDING

by Cynthia Harrod-Eagles

THE FOUNDING, a panoramic saga rich with passion and excitement, launches Dell's most ambitious series to date—THE MORLAND DYNASTY.

From the Wars of the Roses and Tudor England to World War II, THE MORLAND DYNASTY traces the lives, loves and fortunes of a great English family.

A DELL BOOK $3.50   #12677-0